Kaleidoscopic Love

Kaleidoscopic Love

Nikhil Ramesh

PARTRIDGE
A Penguin Random House Company

ISBN:	Hardcover	978-1-4828-5142-7
	Softcover	978-1-4828-5144-1
	eBook	978-1-4828-5143-4

Print information available on the last page.

To order additional copies of this book, contact
Partridge India
000 800 10062 62
orders.india@partridgepublishing.com

www.partridgepublishing.com/india

To my family, with all my heart and soul.

When love is lost, do not bow your head in sadness; instead keep your head up high and gaze into heaven for that is where your broken heart has been sent to heal.

—Author Unknown

PROLOGUE

'Hey, Nikhil, listen to my song that I just recorded. It's from one of the Malayalam movies. Tell me how it is,' Aakash said.

Aakash was my roommate. One of the best guys that I had ever met. Kind and brainy fellow. He had a passion towards singing. He had already contested for a few state-level singing competitions. He used to sing well, I suppose; I don't know heads or tails about singing. Matter of fact, I was bugged up listening to him record his songs every evening when he returned from office.

So I listened to his song. Like I said, I never understood heads or tails about music, but still his recording did sound good to me.

'Aakash, it's nice,' I said. 'Why don't you compose your own song? Write a small script—you know music, you can sing, so why don't you try it?' I said. Aakash said, 'Nik, it's not as easy as you think. Can you do one thing, write a song for me? Actually I wanted to do this earlier. I wanted to compose a song about my love. I shall tell you in brief what happened, and you can write it for me in your own words. What do you say?' 'Err . . . I've never tried writing songs or poems, Aakash, but I can try writing a story, and later on, we can make it short for a song,' I said with a smile. And there it began.

Chapter 1

December 12, 2003

Manipal

Manipal is a university town situated in the state of Karnataka in India. It's a suburb within Udupi City. It's located on the rocky hinterland of the Malabar Coast of south-west India, about eight kilometres from the Arabian Sea. From its location on a plateau, it commands a view of the Arabian Sea to the west, and the Western Ghats range to the east. Buses ply between Manipal and Mangalore every twenty minutes, which is another major city in Karnataka.

The bus that I was travelling on was nearing Manipal, my destination. I started my long journey alone from Mysore. It was my first time in Manipal. As the bus made its way through the city, the place reminded me of my college. I could see lots of colleges around. I saw only a young crowd around. My first impression of Manipal was that the city itself was a huge college campus.

At the very heart of Manipal is Tiger Circle, popularly known as TC by the locals, as I later learnt. All buses and taxis leave from here. It also has a small market with grocery and eateries forming the bulk of shops. The climate was nice; it was winter, so the weather was tropical.

The bus almost reached Tiger Circle, the place where we had decided to meet. My long journey of six hours was coming to an end—or was it just the beginning of another journey? A journey into the unfamiliar.

CHAPTER 2

After two long years of online conversation on Yahoo Messenger, which was a popular chat application back then, and over the phone, I was about to see her for the first time. Until then, I had only seen her in photos that she had sent me. In photos, she wasn't too attractive and sexy. She looked mature and bold. She was studying architecture in the University of Manipal.

The bus had come to a stop. It took me some time to disembark as the bus was filled to its capacity. I was feeling anxious. A lot of things were running through my mind. I was thinking if she would look as I had imagined. I was wondering if she would treat me the same way as I expected. Whether she would like the way I look. Would I disappoint her in any way? Would she spend some time with me or just greet me and return?

I wanted to spend some time with her. It was close to seven o'clock in the evening, and I knew she had to get back to her hostel soon. Her hostel had a strict schedule, and beyond the time, nobody was allowed to get into the hostel. So I wanted to spend some time with her before she returned to her hostel.

With all these shuffled feelings in my mind, I finally stepped out. I looked around and saw a bunch of college students waiting for the bus. I wondered how I would recognize her. I had seen her in photos, but photos can be elusive. It was now time to find out for myself if they were truly hers.

I was looking around left and right, hoping to see somebody whom I could recognize. I glanced to my left again and saw a girl towards the other end of the bus. She was not facing me, so I could not get a better look at her face. But I had sensed that the girl was waiting for someone. I had this strange feeling that she might be the one. But I couldn't get a clear look at her. She was facing towards the opposite side.

Just out of curiosity, I took my phone out of my pocket and quickly dialled her number. I was thinking to myself that if the girl whom I was looking at brought her phone out and received the call, then she was the one. It took a few seconds for the call to connect, and my anxiety level rose with every beep and ring. My thoughts came true when I saw the girl pull out her phone, and just then I heard a click and a hello through my earpiece. The following sentence was in a hurried and tense tone: 'Aakash, where are you?' she asked. In style, I said, 'Turn around.' Like they say, curiosity kills; her looks did kill me. I found myself calling out her name in a very low tone, 'Aasma.' Yes, she was from a different religious community. Aasma means 'precious'.

Do you know what it feels like when a girl holds the stare too long when you least expect it? Have you ever had this feeling as if time were still, a feeling of realization, a rush heading up your spine? For that microsecond, it's as if you don't hear the world around you and you have this tunnel vision.

Boom! And it's broken. You come back to the real world. You start feeling normal, feel your surroundings. But somewhere at the back of your mind, something has been triggered. You don't know what it is until a while later, when you come back to your normal senses and realize that it was the radiance between you and the girl. When our eyes met, it was one of the few times in my life that I felt at a complete loss for words.

She was wearing a pale yellow–coloured salwar. She looked stunning. At twenty-four, she was an exquisite woman. She had fine, delicate features. Eyes light-coloured and soft dark hair. Her skin was fresh and golden. Her figure was stunning, with a gorgeous, firm young body, a small waist, rounded hips, and long, shapely legs. There was a strong sensuality about her. But the magic lay in the fact that beneath the sensuality seemed to lie intelligence and innocence, and the combination was irresistible. Her looks were way beyond my expectations. I stood there spellbound. The photos did not justify her looks. She was looking beautiful. It seemed like everything fit her perfectly. The dress, her long hair that reached her shoulders, and the long, dangling earrings.

Astounded and with all the things going through my mind, I walked towards her. 'How was your journey?' Aasma asked me with a bright smile. The first thing that I noticed is that her voice did not sound the same as I had heard over the phone for so long. It did sound more sweet and shy to me. I told her my journey was good and smooth. After we were done with greeting each other, there was a moment of silence between us. I didn't know what to say next or how to start a conversation. She just kept smiling at me, expecting me to say something. After a moment, I suppose she realized that I wasn't going to start talking. At last she said with her shy smile, 'So . . . shall we . . .' and started to pick up my luggage, which I did not expect a girl to do. I asked her not to pick it up and that I could manage them myself. Aasma insisted that I had to let her carry my bag. Well, I couldn't argue with her over this. I think she wanted to make me feel like a guest, so I let her carry my bag, though I was kind of embarrassed for letting a beautiful girl do it for me. Anyway, my mind was too occupied to say something, so we started walking to the other end of the Tiger Circle towards the rickshaw stand. I didn't even ask her where we were going or why we were going. I quietly followed her.

Silence followed the first moments. I felt somewhat awkward. I thought she might be expecting me to start a conversation. I was searching for a good starting line. Just then, the silence was broken. She looked at me and asked in a shy and pretty direct manner, 'How am I looking, Aakash? How is my dress?' Her question surprised me. I was thinking to myself how I could possibly tell her how magnificent she was looking and how well her dress suited her looks. I could not bring out any word or sentence to express what I felt at that moment. I could only manage to smile.

I think she understood what I had in mind by the smile itself. My smile carried answers to all her questions. She blushed. Slowly, a rosy scarlet colour spread over her cheeks, making her face take on an almost childlike appearance. I didn't see any disappointment in her that I did not answer her question. She smiled back at me. At that moment, I knew that my smile had communicated more to her than if I had uttered a few magical words. She could not hide the glow that came over her face. We continued walking towards the rickshaw stand.

I was still amazed and out of words when we reached the rickshaw stand. During the drive, I felt a bit tired, yet excited and happy that she was sitting beside me. The drive went by in silence. At this point, I was thinking of what might be going through Aasma's mind. What might she be thinking? How might she be feeling? A few minutes later, the rickshaw got off the main road and stopped. I paid for the rickshaw, and we got down. I looked around, and the neighbourhood looked like a well-to-do residential area. I realized that I had not asked her where we were going until now. 'Aasma, where are we heading next?' I asked. 'Relax, Aakash. I've arranged a place for you to stay. My friends have rented a house nearby. You are going to stay with them. You'll enjoy being with them,' she said. She had arranged for a friend's place for me to stay. Well, that was a surprise for me; I had not expected her to arrange a place for me to stay. When I left Mysore, I did not have any idea where I was going to stay or how I was going to manage it. My only thought was to meet Aasma. I had not planned what to do after I was done meeting her. I had no clue as to what I could expect, so I thought it was better I went with the flow, see how the situation unfolded. Nevertheless, I was okay with her plan for now. 'Aasma, it's okay. I'll book a room for myself in any nearby hotel. I don't want to trouble your friends,' I said. 'Quiet. You are my special guest. Come on now. We'll have to walk a bit,' she said.

CHAPTER 3

Her friends' place could be reached only through a narrow way on the other side of the road. We had to cross the wide road. While crossing the road, I happened to hold her hand. I have to say it was not intentional though. While crossing the road, out of my peripheral vision, I did notice that she kept looking at me. I didn't know why she kept looking; she didn't even look at the road for once. I did not realize that I was holding her hand until we reached the other side of the road. When we reached the other side of the road, her eyes were still fixed on me. 'What?' I said. By then I had released her hand. 'You were holding my hand,' she said in a low voice. 'Yeah . . . so . . .' I said. She did not say a word to that, and we started walking down the narrow street.

We reached her friends' place. It was located in V Block, close to Kamath Circle. Aasma introduced me to two boys who were her friends. The boys had rented a two-bedroom house for themselves. They all looked younger than me. One of the boys helped me carry my luggage to the bedroom. After the welcoming, I looked around the house. The room was spacious and comfortable. There was a big, comfy bedstead on one side, a study table and a large mirror on the other. It actually did not look like a boys' bedroom. It was too nice and well maintained to be a boys' room. Anyway, I was happy with the place. I straightaway lay down on the bed. I felt tired and exhausted after the journey. I wanted some quiet time to think and put things together about all that had happened since I had landed in Manipal. How did I manage the happenings till now? How quickly time had slipped away. Things were unfolding unexpectedly. What other surprises would I have?

The knock on the door brought me back from my thoughts. Aasma came in, and I sat up straight to face her. She said in a quick tone, 'Aakash, get ready. We are going out for dinner,' and left the room. Now that was nice. Unlike me, she had planned everything. Wait a minute, what did she mean by 'We are going out for dinner'? Would the other two guys be joining us? I did not like the idea of her friends joining us. I wanted to spend some time alone with her, and I did not want anybody to disturb us. Then I thought it was better not to worry too much about it and let things happen.

I quickly started to freshen up and get dressed. I did not want to waste time getting ready. I had to spend the maximum possible time with her. By the way, I had not brought that many clothes, not expecting a surprise dinner date. I opted to go simple with a light-blue linen shirt, dark denims, and light-tan loafers. I looked kind of casual. I wanted to look better. It was our first date. Well, I couldn't do anything much about it even if I looked like an alien; I just did not have anything else to wear. Standing in front of the mirror, I remembered something my friends used to say: 'When you're wondering what to say or how you look, just remember she's already out with you. That means she said yes when she could have said no. That means she made a plan when she could have just blown you off. So that means it's no longer your job to make her like you. It's your job not to mess it up.'

Aasma was waiting for me outside. 'It seems like the guys have some work to catch up on. They won't be able to join us,' she said. 'So it's just the two of us?' I said. 'Yup,' she said with a naughty wink. I was glad to hear that her friends were not joining us for dinner. I think she had this well planned. She wanted the same, to spend some special time with me.

'There is a restaurant close by called MIT food court. We could take a walk. If you are okay with it,' she said. 'I don't mind. No problem at all. A little walk could do me some help after sitting in the bus for so long,' I said. 'Cool then. Let's go,' she said. I thought it was a nice idea to walk rather than take a rickshaw. It would give us a lot of time to talk. A walk would be sweet. Walk with her, tell her she's pretty, and if all goes well, hold her hand. I'd get to talk to her and find out stuff about her. I thought to myself, *Don't worry about the distance, a kilometre away is fine because it means I have lots of time to talk to her. If she gets tired, she'll probably cling on to me or ask me to carry her there.* Yeah, the idea of such a thing happening gave me chills. My friends used to say that if a girl bumps into your arm while walking with you, she wants you to hold her hand.

Now I was in a dilemma. Do I put my hands in my pocket? Do I leave my hands by my sides? Do I hold out an arm waist-height for her? Which do girls like best? I wanted her to link arms. This was a typical romantic way to walk as a couple without being too touchy-feely.

Guys do like when a girl holds on to our arms while walking. I can't speak for every guy, but I'm pretty sure the majority would agree that men love it when girls hold onto their arms, as long as the girl isn't being ridiculously clingy.

Yes, I adore it! It is a girl's non-verbal way of saying 'I am connected to that person, and that person feels comfortable showing others that he cares for me and enjoys having others know it too.' Sometimes it is romantic, but it's always about connection, which is a great thing.

So we started walking side by side. I put my hands in my pocket. After a few paces, I felt her arm up brush against mine. I didn't know if that was a sign for me to hold her hand, like my friends had told me, or was it just an unintentional body brush? I wasn't sure what to do. Should I hold her hand? What if she jumped back, like she'd just placed her hand on a hot burner, or would she let our bodies linger together for a second if I gave her a smile? If she returned my affection, then she would be welcoming my plan to break the touch barrier. I was thinking that I should keep the first touch casual and friendly to see how she responded. There was no need for a romantic gesture yet. The next thing I realized, she put her arm through mine.

This gave me a weird sensation. I was thinking so much about it and she just made it easy for me. Well, now that's a welcoming sign. So we walked with our arms linked.

She looked up and said, 'I can see a lot of stars today. The sky is so clear. It's nice, isn't it . . . ?' 'Yeah, that's because I am here,' I said as if it was a cool thing to say. 'From now on, every time I see so many stars in the sky, I'll remember this moment,' she said. 'What can I say? I hope you always remember me the same way,' I said. She tightened her grip on my arm, stepped a bit closer, and rested her head on my shoulders. By the time I could respond, she backed off. I think she thought it was too much for now. I looked up, thought to myself, *Never mind how many stars, this moment feels awesome*, and our romantic walk continued till the restaurant.

CHAPTER 4

The food court was designed to attract. It looked great from outside, but inside it was even better. It had a large seating area. We sat across each other and ordered shawarma. The restaurant was filled with people. I could see a cricket match being played on the screen across the table. So I watched the match for some time then switched to look at her, then back to the television.

So we were on this date, and she started talking about how her family was the same as the decimal system, and how, as she was sure I could imagine, this made it harder for her to . . . do something. I don't really remember. I wasn't paying attention. I was more concerned with what I was going to say next, trying to come up with some clever on-deck topics of conversation. My anxiety spiked as I tried to think of something original to say, something that would indicate I was charming, intelligent, and witty, but I would have settled for simply 'not a moron'. The dish arrived; we both were hungry, and we finished it pretty much in silence. I think the place was crowded, so we did not try to talk much. We left the place soon after. From the restaurant we took a rickshaw back to her hostel. I was looking out, thinking to myself that this pleasant time was coming to an end. I did not realize that it had been four or five hours since I had landed in Manipal. Time was flying. I think now I did realize Einstein's theory of relativity. Wondered if even Einstein had a girl who made him come up with the theory. Anyway I was wishing that we would reach her hostel late. I wished the rickshaw to be a bit slow. We sat close to each other holding hands. She got close to me. There was hardly any distance between us. There was silence. A sense of fear. A sense of love. Her eyes spoke a lot.

Aasma. I talked to her. I cared for her. Our relationship was moving fast. Now I was in a rickshaw with her so close that hardly any air passed between us. We were both staring at each other, and before I could say anything, she kissed me on the cheek. Her kiss sent chills through my body. Surprised for the moment, I did not react to it. She quickly pulled away and gave me a shy glance.

I did not know if she expected me to kiss her back. But I thought, *We are travelling in a rickshaw, and it might not seem good if I kissed her back.*

We reached the front gate of her hostel. She said something that I did not expect her to say. She said, 'When I leave, I won't turn back.' Her statement confused me to the core. 'What do you mean?' I asked. 'When I leave, if I turn back and look at you, you will miss me and even I will be thinking of you and miss you. So it is better we don't look at each other when we leave. I'll give you a call once I reach my hostel room. Okay?' she said. I managed to say 'Alright.' She left, and the rickshaw started to move. I was peeping out the rickshaw to see her if she turned back, but she didn't.

I reached her friends' place. I changed and was ready to sleep. Her friends made me feel as comfortable as possible. The boys were nice. We spoke for some time, getting to know each other. Then we all thought we'd watch a movie. They played some English movie. I couldn't concentrate on the movie. My mind was still busy thinking about her. I was lost in thoughts. After a while, Aasma called me. We spoke for another two hours. I told her that I was missing her and I missed the good time that we had.

She told me that she was going to Kerala with her aunt the next day and then to Dubai. I was disappointed and felt really sad that I was going to miss her. It was quite late in the night when our conversation ended. I went to bed, but I couldn't sleep. For another couple of hours I kept thinking. I was thinking about my journey till now. How all this started and where I was now. I don't know when I drifted into sleep.

The next morning, I was the first one to wake up. I felt like I had not slept at all. I called Aasma and told her that I would pick her up from her hostel. I had to go to Mysore.

CHAPTER 5

Aasma had booked a flight to Dubai from Kerala two days later. From Manipal we had to go to Mangalore, and from Mangalore, Aasma had to catch a train to Kerala. So I thought, *I can accompany her till Mangalore. From there, I can even get a train to Mysore.* Though Mysore trains are always booked, and it is hard to find an unreserved seat, I decided to give it a try.

I went to her hostel. She was there waiting for me near the front gate. She was wearing a pale-orange salwar. She was looking pretty. 'Hey, good morning. You look pretty today,' I said. 'Hey, thanks.' She blushed. 'There is a place called Dollops near Tiger Circle. We can have breakfast there. We'll take a rickshaw,' she said. So we picked our bags and took a rickshaw to Tiger Circle. It was a five-minute drive.

On the way, she started telling me about the place. 'Dollops is hidden in a small corner of Tiger Circle. The place has good food and is a favourite with the student population. There are often people waiting for tables. The food is good, and the menu has a lot of variety. Nice ambience and good music as well.'

We reached Dollops and found a table for ourselves. 'Aakash, I like eggs. Shall we order something with egg?'

she said. So we ordered bread and egg. We finished our breakfast quickly. We were supposed to meet Aasma's aunt who was going with her to Kerala. Her aunt would come to her hostel. We had to take a rickshaw back to her hostel.

By the time we reached the hostel, her aunt was already there waiting. Aasma introduced me to her aunt. It was very formal and short. We had to reach the Manipal bus stand now. We took the same rickshaw by which we came. The drive was pretty uncomfortable. Me first, Aasma at the far end, and her aunt in the middle, blocking us from any further conversation. Three of us reached the Manipal bus stand. We boarded the bus to Mangalore. I think her aunt did make out that we were quite close and we needed privacy, so she took a seat in the front row, and we sat three rows behind her. Seated holding each other's hands with fingers intertwined, we waited for the bus to move.

I thought it might not look good when people saw us sitting close and holding hands, so I let go of her hand. The bus started towards Mangalore. After a couple of minutes, I wanted to ask her something. But I didn't know how to ask her, how to start. Was it the time to ask her, or if I missed this opportunity, would I get another chance to ask her? I did not want to risk missing this opportunity, because you never know if you will get another chance. With all the thoughts racing in my mind, I could feel the lump form in my throat. Finally I managed to gather enough courage to ask her, 'Aasma, will you marry me?'

My heart began to beat faster. I was breathing heavily. I could hear my heartbeat echoing throughout my head. The closer I got to the moment, the more nervous I became.

I could feel the rush inside me, waiting for her answer. She just gave me a smile and said, 'Am from a different community.' 'So what?' I asked. She just shook her head and gripped my hand with a gentle squeeze. It was a confusing and unclear message. I could not understand if the gesture was yes or anything else.

I asked her again, 'Will you marry me?' She looked at me and said, 'It is not going to happen, Aakash. It is not practical.' I didn't know how to react to it. I just smiled and did not speak any further.

An hour later, we reached the Mangalore bus stand. The railway station was a few minutes' drive from there. We took a rickshaw, and again it was an uncomfortable ride. I was sitting on one side, Aasma was sitting on the other side, and her aunt was in the middle. I felt like in a few minutes she would be leaving, and I wanted to talk to her, but because of her aunt in the middle, I could not speak.

We reached the railway station. Aasma had already booked the tickets, so we didn't have to stand and wait in the long queue for the tickets. We had a few minutes' time before the train left. I was upset that she was leaving and that I could not complete our conversation that started in the bus. Aasma came close to me and gently touched my face. Her soft thin and long fingers caressed my face. It felt so nice and romantic. 'Don't worry. I'll be back soon,' she said. I thought this would be the last time I would see her.

She boarded the train, found a place to sit for herself and her aunt. She put down the luggage, came and stood near the door. She took my hand in hers, and the train started to move slowly. I held her hand and walked with the slow-moving train for a few seconds. Then the train picked up pace, and I had to let go of her hand. We said good-bye to each other.

I stood there for a long time even after the train had passed. I went to the ticket counter to check if there were seats available for Mysore. The train to Mysore would usually be crowded. I did not have a reservation, so getting an unreserved seat was difficult. Fortunately I got a ticket, but with the ticket, I just had to hope that I could find a seat for myself. I looked at my watch. The next train was scheduled to arrive in two hours from now. So I had to wait. I sat on a bench close by, and I could not get my mind off her. With a lot of things in my mind—confusion, sadness—I finally summoned up the courage to message her, 'I love you, Aasma.'

I felt like time had slowed down as I waited for her reply. Each minute felt like an hour. But the good thing is that I didn't have to wait for a long time for her to reply. She replied, 'I love you too! I miss you so much, and I want you close to me. But I don't know what to do.' Finally, I felt a sense of relief. I felt like jumping and screaming, but I thought better of it. I didn't want to make a joker of myself in public. After a while, I saw that my messages were not being delivered. I tried calling her, but she was out of coverage area. I sat on the bench close by, thinking about her.

The train to Mysore arrived on time. I ploughed my way through the crowd and got into the train. I quickly went from one carriage to another searching for a seat. It would be a long journey to Mysore, so I had to find a comfortable place. Searching for a seat, I was almost nearing the tail end of the train. Finally I saw an empty seat at the far end of the carriage. I quickly went and caught hold of it. I hurriedly kept my luggage on the overhead carrier and sat down. Gosh . . . my bottom felt like I was sitting on a rock. It was an old-style wooden seat. I could not imagine how hard the journey would be. A long journey and a wooden seat. I thought by the time I reached Mysore, my bottom would have become as hard as the wooden seat itself.

CHAPTER 6

The long journey to Mysore just passed by while daydreaming about Aasma and how things would be in future. Everything and every part of my life would change.

Back home in Mysore that night, I was really able to recollect everything that happened in the past few days. It began as a thrilling idea to meet somebody for the first time, and I thought about how the events turned out to be an emotional adventure and where the whole thing stood right now. When I started off, I never realized that this may become serious.

My phone beeped, a message from Aasma: 'Reached home. Missing you.' I quickly replied back, 'Miss you too,' but the message was not delivered. Maybe the network was poor in her area. A while later, my phone buzzed; it was Aasma calling. I quickly picked up the call. She had promised me that she would call me after reaching home. The conversation continued about how much she was missing me. I also expressed how I felt, and my mind was transported to a different world. I remember my mom calling me a few times for dinner. I was too occupied to have dinner also. We both talked until the early hours next day. Don't ask me what we spoke about almost the whole night. Maybe it was something silly or senseless. We just wanted to talk to each other.

I woke up late the next morning. My parents were unaware of the recent events. Mom was behind me, enquiring about my long phone call last night. They were surprised to see me on the phone for such a long time. I gave them a vague answer that it was my friend and quickly left the place before they had a chance to ask me any more questions. I wanted to talk to Aasma again. I called her but could not connect. Network problem again.

I did not try calling her again. I was waiting for her to call when she was able to. I did not want to disturb her while she was busy packing her stuff. I didn't want her to blame me for forgetting something, as girls usually do. Meanwhile I did not have anything else to do other than sitting home and recalling everything that happened in the past few days. So I thought of catching up with my friends. That could help me stay grounded. I dressed up and went to our hang-out place. It was a small tea shop with a couple of chairs and a long bench. All my friends usually spend time there talking about all the latest news and hot new girls in the vicinity. I met my friend Sam there. He was one of my close friends. We were in the same class, and we were staying in the same neighbourhood. Sam was surprised to see me. 'Where were you, lost yesterday and the day before? You didn't receive my call at all. What happened?' he asked. He was surprised that I had disappeared suddenly for three days and did not receive his call. Usually this would not be the case. We used to go to college together; the same classes meant bunking together, same friends, same neighbourhood. On the whole, I and Sam were together for the most part of the day. So he had a good reason to be surprised and upset about it. Things had happened so fast that I never got a chance to tell him about anything in the past few days. I just smiled. I did not want to tell anybody about what had happened. At least until things were solid. If I told my friends now, they would start teasing me and comment about it. They would think I was crazy. To my relief, a couple of friends came in; we greeted each other, and Sam did not continue with the topic.

I was in such a happy mood that I ordered tea and biscuits for all my friends. I had nothing else to do till evening when Aasma would call me. Until then, let me spend some time with friends. Boys were talking about the latest car, its features and prices. Some were talking about the new chick in the next street, her name and other things that boys usually talk about. But none of these interested me now. I was still thinking about Aasma. I just wanted the day to end. I so desperately wanted to tell somebody how I was feeling. Sam hit me on my shoulder and asked, 'What, Aakash, you are in a good mood today. You look happy today. What happened? Did your parents give you too much pocket money today?' 'Err . . . nothing as such. Just feeling good today,' I said. He turned his attention to the topic of the new girl. My mom started calling me. I did not answer. I knew that it was lunchtime and she was waiting for me.

I came home later for lunch. Mom had prepared chicken, my favourite. Again I was too occupied to even enjoy my favourite food. I had my lunch watching TV for the latest news and new inventions. I slept for a while after lunch. I knew that Aasma would call me late at night, and I did not want to sleep while talking to her.

That night, Aasma called me. 'Hey, Aakash, how are you? How is everything over in Mysore?' she asked me. 'Everything is going good,' I said.

'Hey, listen, I won't be able to talk to you much. I have a lot of things to pack. I am leaving for Dubai tomorrow evening. And by the way, my aunt was curious about you. She was asking too many questions about you. I let out a small clue that we like each other. I did not tell her much, though, just enough for her to understand. She might be of help for us in future,' she said with a giggle. 'All right, let's see. Hope she doesn't complain about it to your parents,' I said.

'Okay then, I will call you from the airport before leaving. Take care.'

'Take care.'

So that was a brief call. I spent the rest of the night watching TV, and I don't remember when I slept.

I woke up the next morning to go to college. It felt as if it had been a long time since I had gone to college, like the way you feel when you go to school after a long summer vacation. I picked up Sam on the way from his place. We were close buddies. He was my classmate in college. Every day we used to go to college together, and most of the time, we were together. Apart from Sam, Felix and Vachan were in my close group of friends in college.

On the way to the college, Sam again asked me, 'Aakash, where have you been in the last few days? I am just curious. This is the first time you have gone out without even telling me anything. What happened? Is everything okay?' 'Yes, buddy, nothing much. I went to my aunt's place in Mangalore. It was a sudden plan, so I couldn't tell you,' I said. 'Oh, I don't remember you telling me anything about your aunt in Mangalore. Is it a new aunt? Don't lie, Aakash. You're a bad liar,' he said. 'Err . . . tell you what, I have been to Mangalore to meet a girl,' I said. 'A girl? Aakash, you and a girl? I don't believe it. Tell me more about it. Who is that girl, did you go alone?' he asked. 'Boy, you have too many questions. Let's go to the college first, I'll tell you the whole story,' I said.

We met Felix and Vachan in the college. Our first class was about to start in a few minutes. 'Let's go have a coffee first,' Vachan said. So we went to a tea shop nearby. That was our usual hang-out place when we weren't attending classes, and frankly, we didn't attend that many classes. As we ordered coffee and tea, Sam said, 'Boys, listen to this new story—Aakash has been to Mangalore to meet a girl. He didn't tell anybody about it.' Now everybody turned to look at me. 'Is that so? What happened? Who is that girl? Tell us something about it?' Felix asked. 'Sam, this is why I didn't want to tell you about this. You'd start spreading the news,' I said. 'It's okay, buddy. What is the harm in telling us? Come on,' Sam said.

Now that my friends were curious, I told them about Aasma, how it had started, how we met, and what happened in Mangalore. And when I ended, everyone was surprised.

'So what next? What are you going to do next?' Felix asked. 'I am not sure. I couldn't talk to her properly yesterday. I am waiting for her call,' I said.

'Alright, let's go to college. Let's attend at least one class in a day,' I said.

'Aakash, do you have her photo?' Sam whispered in the middle of the lecture. I was not really listening to what the lecturer was teaching. My mind was occupied. I just wanted the day to end and go home and call Aasma. 'No, buddy. I don't have her photo now,' I said. 'At least show me her profile on Orkut,' he said. 'Alright, I'll go home and show you,' I said.

'Hey, guys, am not feeling like attending any more classes. I'll go home and rest,' I said after the class ended. 'Hey, drop me near the IS building, I'll meet my friend there,' Sam said. So I dropped Sam and went home.

'Hey, you are home early. What happened? No classes today?' Mom asked me. 'No, the lecturer is sick, it seems. No classes today,' I said and went straight to watch TV.

In the evening, as promised, Aasma called me. 'Hey, Aakash, I am about to board the flight. I'll message you my new number as soon as I get one in Dubai,' she said. 'All right, have fun. Don't forget to message. I'll be waiting,' I said. 'I'll miss you, Aakash.' 'I'll miss you too, bye.'

***

Three days later, I got a call from an unknown number. It looked like an international number. Right away I knew it was Aasma calling me.

'Aakash, listen quick, I don't have much balance. This is my new number. Call me when possible. I am going out with my parents. I can't talk to you today,' Aasma said. 'Alright, thanks. I'll call you tomorrow. Bye.'

***

I called her the next evening, and we spoke for a few minutes. She told me about the new mall that she had been to yesterday. It was another brief talk. When I was done with the call, I saw that the few-minutes' call had cost me almost my entire month's phone bill allowance. The call charges were quite expensive. With this kind of call rate, I thought I could call her only once or twice in a month at most. I needed much more daily allowance from my parents. And what reason would I give them? They would certainly ask me a hundred questions, and even still I was not sure if they would give it to me. I needed money badly, and as a student, I had no income. I had to plan something for a few thousand bucks now.

The next morning, I had a plan for it. I would tell my parents that I was going to join tuition classes for one of the subjects and that I needed money for tuition fee. Anyway, I would be out with friends every evening, so it wouldn't be difficult to answer when my dad asked me if I was attending classes every evening. In about two months, I could ask for tuition fee again, and I knew that my fake initial tuition money will not last for long. I would need money again after two months. And to make it quick, I had to tell my parents that the last date to pay the fee was coming up soon.

I convinced my parents that I had to join extra classes if I had to clear my examinations. As expected, they asked me a hundred questions for over an hour. I think they weren't entirely convinced, but they agreed to pay.

I went to my room and let out a sigh of relief. I would have the money in the next few days, and then I could call

Aasma again. In the meantime, there was no message or call from Aasma.

***

The next few days passed by quickly. Not much action in college. I was not in the mood to attend dull lectures. I went to go home early, watched TV, and hung out with friends in the evening.

I got the money from my dad. I was so happy to see it that I had to control myself from smiling wide. Dad would wonder why I was so happy to attend extra classes when I was not attending the lectures in college. He would ask me a hundred more questions, and that was something I wanted to avoid. I said, 'I'll go complete the admission formalities right away,' and quickly left home to renew my call balance. I recharged for a thousand bucks with international calling tariff. Never had I recharged for a large amount. It's funny to say, but now my phone was more precious for me. It felt like it weighed more now after the recharge, not literally though.

I went to our usual tea shop in our neighbourhood. I thought, *I'll have a hot tea and call Aasma*. Sam and a couple of friends were already there. After the pleasantries, I had a hot cup of tea and called Aasma. She did not answer. I called her again but no answer. I tried five times, but she did not answer me. I was upset. 'Hey, Aakash, who are you calling?' Sam asked. 'Nothing, just a friend,' I said.

My phone beeped, a message from Aasma.

'Hey, Aakash, sorry, I was out with parents so couldn't answer. Call me now if you are free.'

I called her, and we spoke for a few minutes. I tried to keep the conversation brief. I wanted my currency balance to last long, not finish it in a day. It was another brief talk. Nothing new going on with her in Dubai. Nothing new here as well except that I spent less time attending college lectures and watching TV more at home or hanging out with friends.

CHAPTER 7

In the initial days when Aasma went to Dubai, I called her every day and spoke for a few minutes. As days passed, the frequency of calls decreased. I couldn't manage my phone currency to last long enough, and I could not ask my parents for more tuition fee every few weeks. Our conversations were not exciting anymore. I had to look for a new topic every time I called her just to keep up the conversation. Nothing new in Dubai and my routine life back here.

After about a month and a half, Aasma called me quite early in the morning. She was sounding exasperated. 'Aakash, you remember my aunt in Mangalore? She called my mom last night, and it seems like she spilled her guts about us. My parents are questioning me as if I am a criminal. They are driving me mad. I can't hold it back for long. I am locked up in my room. What shall I do now?' 'Relax, Aasma. Wait a minute. I will call you back,' I said and disconnected. I quickly washed my face just so that I would be totally awake. I needed a minute to two to think about this. This had to be handled carefully or things could become chaotic and I might get into trouble. I had no idea how her parents were or how exactly her dad was. He might call up somebody in India and have me beaten up badly. First I had to know about her parents—what questions they asked her, how they were reacting. If I had answers to these questions, I may be able to tell her what to do. Well, somewhere at the back of my mind I knew that I would ask her to tell her parents the truth and hope that they were convinced.

A few minutes later, I called Aasma. I asked her during the call the questions that I had. It seems like her father was furious about her getting involved with a guy when she was supposed to be concentrating on her studies. Her parents were quite rich, and her father was quite influential. He had good contacts. He wanted to know everything that had happened. I told Aasma to tell the truth to her parents and try to convince them. She was crying and reluctant to tell her parents. She thought her parents would never allow something like this to happen. Finally she agreed to what I said. She said she would call me back after some time. I disconnected the call and waited to hear the outcome.

The whole day, I was completely upset by what was happening. Everything was happening so fast. Did I really want to get involved in this? I had heard stories of such things happening and that these things usually were the case when you love somebody. I thought to go with the flow for now and think of things as they happened. I did not attend college that day. I spent my entire day in the coffee shop. In the evening, I went to Sam's place. He asked me why I looked so upset, and I told him what had happened. He reminded me that I had not shown Aasma's photo to him. I opened Orkut and showed him Aasma's profile.

'Hey, she is good-looking. How did she even fall for you so soon? Anyway, you make a nice couple,' he said. 'Yeah, let's hope everything turns out good,' I said.

Later that night, Aasma sent me a message.

'I want to talk to you. Call me late at night.'

'Okay.'

I watched TV until late in the night. I knew the time zone. Dubai was one and half hour behind, so I called up quite late in the night.

'Hello,' she whispered. She sounded like she was still crying.

'Tell me what happened. Did you tell your parents about us? What did they say?' I asked.

'Yes, I told them that you were from Bangalore. But I told them the truth about the rest of the things. They are quite mad at me. They said that they will look for a boy and get me married soon if I am going to continue this,' she said. 'Relax, that is expected. Every parent would say this,' I said. 'Dad had some important work, so he couldn't talk to me. They will talk about this again tomorrow morning. I want to come back to India,' she said. 'Alright, talk to your parents again tomorrow morning. Message or call me after that. I'll be waiting,' I said.

'Okay. Good night.' She disconnected the call.

I just lay on my bed and kept imagining what might happen and how things could turn out. What if my parents got to know about it? How would they react? I drifted into sleep.

***

The next morning, I woke up late. The first thing I did when I woke up was to check if I had any message from Aasma. There was no call or message from her yet. My mom was screaming that I was late for college. I quickly dressed up and called Sam to tell him that I'd be late. By the time I reached the college, I had missed the first two classes. I attended the next two, went to the coffee shop with friends, and spent some time there. Vachan told me that the lecturer was asking about me and why I was not attending classes regularly. 'Chuck it. I have my own problems to take care of. I will take care of classes later,' I said. I went home after finishing my coffee. I just wanted to be alone now. I was waiting to hear from Aasma.

Later in the evening, I called her several times; she did not answer any of my calls. I left her a few messages asking what had happened and why she was not receiving my call. I got no response. Later when I tried, her phone was switched off.

***

Days passed, months passed, but there was no news from Aasma. Every time I tried, her phone was switched off. She never called me after that. It had been three months, and I knew that by now she would be back in India. I also kept checking her profile online to see if there was any activity. But her profile seemed inactive for a long time.

I was completely disturbed by this. I did not know if she was in trouble or if she was okay. Did she get married? How could she do that? What about her feelings for me? What about all the things that she had promised me? Did it not matter anymore to her? I did not try to contact her anymore. I just wanted to get away from all this for a while. I had lost my interest in studies, my family and friends. I thought it was better to have people who cared about me rather than any good-looking girl who did not even bother about me.

My friends asked me from time to time about Aasma and how things were going between us. I said I had lost contact with her and I didn't want to talk about her any further. I think they understood and left it at that.

My life gradually came back to normal. I started attending classes regularly. I spent some good time with friends that I had lost touch with in the past and quality time with family. I now wanted to be surrounded by people. I did not want to be left alone. I knew I would think about Aasma if I was alone, and I had to get her out of my mind. I had to forget her. I felt it was good that things had ended quickly rather than much later on. That would have hurt a lot more.

CHAPTER 8

1.5 Years Later

My life was back to normal. It had been several months since I had lost touch with Aasma, in fact, more than a year or so. I did not think of her anymore nor did I have any feelings left for her anymore. Old Aakash was back.

I cleared all my exams, and I was happy that I made it after all the upsets. We had another month or so until the next semester started.

I and my college friends planned for a short trip to a nearby place. It was a three-hour bike ride. I had collected a small amount out of my daily pocket money. We planned to stay in a resort for a night and return the next morning. That weekend, four of us on two bikes started off for the short trip to a nearby hill station. I loved travelling. It was cold, and I thoroughly enjoyed the scenic ride. We did stop by several times to take pictures and for hot coffee. It was a much-needed break in the cold ride, even though we had jackets and gloves on.

We reached the resort. It was in the middle of a tea estate. Everywhere you looked, there were only hills covered in tea plantations. We dropped our luggage in the resort, and we visited a few well-known places in the afternoon. By evening we were ready for a campfire and a nice hot dinner. It was cold, so everybody decided to have a drink. We ordered a bottle of whiskey.

It was quite late in the night when we finished our dinner and prepared for bed. I was a little high, so I lay on bed fiddling with my mobile and drifted to sleep.

The next morning, everybody woke up early. I checked the time on my phone. There was a call from my mom and another message. I called my mom and told her that we were safe and would be returning by evening. I checked the message. It was from an unknown number. It read 'Aakash, I still love you. I don't know what happened to me back then.' I knew it could only be Aasma's message. I quickly checked the conversation. I could not find the start of it. I checked in Sent Items. Apparently I had sent a message to Aasma last night while I was high. She had replied from another number, and the conversation had continued. What a stupid thing I had done. Why did I even message her? I felt like beating myself up. I shouldn't have messaged her. I had completely forgotten about everything that had happened. I had removed her from my life. What was I thinking? I did not want to get involved in this again. It was like deliberately jumping into trouble. But then, somewhere in the bottom of my heart, I felt happy that she still loved me. She may not have hurt me on purpose. Something must have made her do it. She still loved me, and that was all that mattered. I would forgive her for everything if she said just once that she loved me. I realized that I still had feelings for her, but I had intentionally boxed them up. I felt my love for her reviving. I thought it was not a good idea to call or message her. I had messaged last night while I was high. She might also be playing me. If she really loved me, she would call me again. Until then, I would not message her. I wanted to enjoy the trip, not let this matter ruin my trip.

That evening, we returned back to Mysore. Mom prepared coffee for me and asked me about the trip. I told her about the beautiful hills. I said I would show her the photos. I had to load the photos to my computer and post them online. I had a bunch of good photos of the scenery and my friends. I thought I would rest for some time and work on the photos next morning.

The next morning, I woke up early. I transferred the photos from my phone to my computer. I was really glad that we had made that trip. I had such memorable photos of my friends. I knew that we would go our ways after graduating. But I would cherish these memories. I posted some of the photos online. Soon after I posted the photos online, people started posting comments. It was really nice to see. I wished that we friends could stay the same forever. Only two more years of our college were ahead, and in time, we would gradually drift apart, and surely by the end of the final semester, we would part ways in search of jobs.

I was about to close when a message popped up in the social networking site. It was Aasma. She was online today.

'Hey u there?'

'Yup,' I replied.

'What happened, you did not call or message me. I was waiting.'

'Waiting for what?'

'Two days back, you were chatting with me the entire night, and suddenly you stopped. I thought you didn't want to continue. I was waiting for your reply,' she said.

'Nothing, I just drifted to sleep. So didn't reply."

'Okay.'

'Am sorry Aakash. I still love you.'

I didn't know what to respond. Part of me wanted to say 'I love you too' and part of me did not want to get involved again.

'?? Please answer me Aakash. Don't you love me anymore? I said am sorry.'

'Love you too. I'll call you later,' I replied.

I knew that I was flying into trouble zone, but partly I was happy to have her back. I shut down my system and dressed up for college.

I was in a happy mood. I thought I would keep this a secret, and till I was sure things were back on track, I would not even tell my friends. I attended all the classes that day. That evening, Aasma messaged me from her new number.

'U busy? Call me when you are free. I need to tell you something.'

I did not respond to it. It feels nice when a girl gives you so much attention. I wanted that to happen for a few more days. I thought I would show some disinterest now, just to gain some more attention.

'Will you call me tonight?' she messaged again. I did not respond to it. I thought not to respond until I called her late in the night.

After dinner, I watched TV for some time. I had to call Aasma, so I did not want to sleep. Late at night again, she gave me a missed call. I had my mobile charging. She had left a message.

'Are you going to call or shall I sleep?'

I thought if I pushed it too much, even she would think that I had lost interest in her and I was playing with her. She may not message me again. So I called her. She picked up before the first ring ended.

'Hello, Aakash,' she said.

'Hey, how are you? Long time.'

'I'm fine,' she said.

'You wanted to tell me something?' I asked.

'Yes, I wanted to tell you that I am sorry,' she said.

'That's okay.'

'But I still want to know how come you suddenly replied to me. I tried to talk to you so many times, I left so many messages. You didn't respond to them. What happened now?" I asked.

'After I told everything about us to my parents, for two whole days, my mom talked me out of it. In the end, I actually felt what they were telling was right. I should be concentrating on my studies first and then think about this later on,' she said.

'Then why are you talking to me now?' I asked angrily.

'Because I can continue to concentrate on my studies and still be with you. I was thinking of changing my college,' she said.

'Which college are you going to join?'

'I will continue my studies in your college so we can be together and study together. My parents don't know that you are from Mysore. I have told them that you are from Bangalore. I will tell them that your college is better and I can score well if I continue my studies in your college,' she said.

'Will your parents agree to it?' I asked.

'Yes, I think so. If I can convince them,' she said.

'Changing college is not as easy as you think, Aasma. There are a lot of formalities,' I said.

'Yes, I know that. I will take care of it. My dad has contacts,' she said.

'Where are you going to stay? How are you going to manage?' I asked.

'My uncle stays in Mysore. I will stay with them. No problem at all. I will talk to my parents about this tomorrow morning,' she said.

'Okay then, call me tomorrow. Goodnight.' I disconnected.

I stayed awake for a long time that night. I was imagining how it might be if I and Aasma were in the same college. How exciting it would be to go to college every day. I could see her every day and attend class as well. My studies would also not be affected. If we both had free time, we could go out to some place or spend time in the nearby café. How nice it would be.

I was thinking that I should not be calling her every day. I wanted to take things slow this time.

***

Two days later, Aasma called me. 'Hey, I spoke to my parents. They have agreed to it. I will be joining your college soon enough. My dad also spoke to my uncle in Mysore. Everything is being arranged,' she said.

'Hey, that's nice,' I said. 'So when will you be shifting to Mysore?'

'Maybe in another two weeks, I guess,' she said.

'That's cool,' I said.

So she really was serious about this. She was going to join our college. What was she up to? What has happened to her suddenly? The next two weeks just passed by. I called her twice in a week or thrice at most and talked mostly about unimportant things.

Finally it was about time. She was shifting to Mysore tomorrow. She had called me the night before. Her uncle would be helping her. She said she would call me once everything was set in Mysore. She may be joining our college in about a week or so.

CHAPTER 9

The thought of Aasma studying in our college actually excited me. How people might feel about the new beauty in college. How they might react when they got to know that she was my—you know, whatever. My friends had forgotten about her. It was nice to imagine that one of the hot girls in college was with me. Every boy who had been going around good-looking girls—oh, I wanted to see the looks on their faces when they heard about me and Aasma.

That weekend, Aasma called me and told me that she would be joining college the next day. 'How are you going to commute? Do you have plans of buying a vehicle?' I asked. 'For now, I'll commute by bus. I'll have to ask my parents to buy me a new vehicle soon. My aunt says there is a bus stop very close by and the bus facility is very good,' she said. She asked me many questions about our college. She was curious to know everything. 'You first come to college, you will get to know,' I said.

After I was done talking to her, I searched through my wardrobe for some of the best T-shirts. I wanted to look good. I wanted her to think that I was one of the best-looking guys in college. I had to buy new ones very soon. I selected the best T-shirt and jeans that I was going to wear the next day. The last time we met was in Mangalore. This would be the first time we would meet in Mysore.

***

The next morning, I woke up early. I couldn't sleep well the previous night though. I was so excited and imagining about the next day. I don't remember what I was imagining about. Like every guy madly in love, my mind was just wandering from one place to other. I hurriedly dressed up and reached college earlier than usual. I was in a blissful mood. I was waiting to see Aasma. I wasn't sure where I could find her. I thought of calling her, but then I thought it was better to wait for her to call. She would definitely call me when she was in college. She might not have reached there yet. In the meantime, I went to the tea shop. I met Felix and Vachan there.

By the time we left the tea shop, our first class was soon to begin. I was about to call Aasma when I saw the lecturer approaching the classroom. I couldn't call her. I was wondering if she may feel bad if I didn't meet her on her first day in college. She had no friends here; she didn't know anybody in our college. I should have at least met her first and helped her find the classroom just to make her comfortable—or was I just looking for a reason to meet her?

After the first lecture ended, I called Aasma. She didn't answer my call. I tried again and no response. I thought she may have already started attending classes. But why didn't she call me when she came to college? I left the classroom to go around the building and the campus to see if I could find her anywhere.

I looked around most of the campus. I passed by most of the classrooms, trying to peek in through the window to see if she was in any of them. I was hoping I could get a glimpse of her. After a half hour, I did not see any sign of her. I called her again; she did not answer. By now the whole campus was kind of empty. All the students were either attending classes or out of the campus. I thought it was better not to get caught by the principal or a lecturer this way. I did not want to run into trouble. I left the college campus and went to a tea shop. All my friends were attending the classes. I ordered tea and thought I would wait for the next hour.

I waited until all the classes were finished and the college gates were closed. I had finished about ten or eleven cups of tea until evening. I did not have lunch either. Before leaving college, I called her again. I was actually disappointed about the whole day. I had expected a lot, and nothing had happened the entire day.

I went home. Mom prepared tea and snacks for me. Mom asked, 'Why are you so silent? Did something happen in college? Is everything fine?' 'Yeah, am fine. Nothing happened. Just a little tired today,' I said. I changed and left to meet Sam. I just wanted to be occupied now.

***

Sam was busy with his mobile when I reached his place. It was his usual thing to call up every other girl he knew and talk to them the whole night long. I was browsing through the Internet when my phone beeped. Aasma was calling me.

'Hello,' I said in an irritated tone.

'Aakash.'

'Tell me, Aasma,' I said.

'Why were you peeping through all the classrooms today?' she said. I could feel that she was grinning. All my disappointment and annoyance just vanished in a nanosecond. So she *was* in class today; she did see me. That was a relief.

'Whom were you searching for?' she asked, though she knew the answer to it.

'I was looking for my friend,' I said.

'Which friend? Is it a girl or a boy?' she asked, trying to tease me.

'Stop it, Aasma. You know I was looking for you. You told me that you will be calling me once you reached college. You neither called me nor answered my call. Which is your classroom?' I asked.

'I won't tell you. You find out. And I just wanted to see how curious you would be to meet me today. That is why I did not call you.'

'What logic is that?' I asked.

'You won't understand. I'll meet you tomorrow,' she said and disconnected.

***

I spent some time roaming around with Sam. I was feeling fine after talking to her. I was excited again. I was imagining on the next level. I was feeling excited about the unexpected after an entire day of nothing but disappointment. I had to search for another good outfit to wear tomorrow. Maybe I would have to borrow a cool-looking eye gear from Sam.

Next morning, I woke up with the same excitement. Fully dressed, I reached college along with Sam. Again, I was a little early to college. I dropped off Sam and went to roam around the college on my bike. I crossed almost all the approach roads to our college. People used to call it 'beat around the college'. After passing through all the roads, still no sign of her. I thought, *From which road will she be coming?* I knew that she would be coming by bus, and I had also passed by the bus stop a few times, but I did not see her. I thought it was better to wait in the college campus and meet her when she calls. Well, I didn't go to college; instead I went straight to the tea shop.

Two hours later, she called me. By now I had missed two morning classes waiting in the tea shop. I received her call. She said that she had free time and would meet me in the college campus. I went back to college and parked my bike near the entrance. Usually all the college students in their free time would spend time in the eatery or the fresh juice shop around the college. Guys would show off on their bikes to the girls present.

I sat on my bike as if I were posing for a photo shoot with the eye gear on that I had borrowed from Sam. From the entrance, I had the view of even the last building in our college campus. I was intensely watching each of the building entrances. It seemed like it was free time for many classes, and too many people were going out of the college campus. My view of the building entrance was constantly being obstructed. Some people whom I knew came and spoke to me. I was, perhaps, not interested in talking to them. I just wished them a good day and turn to look at the crowd.

In the middle of the crowd, at last I saw her. Aasma. I silently let out a sigh. I just couldn't take my eyes off her. She wasn't as dressed up as I expected. She was wearing a simple pale-yellow top and blue jeans and heeled footwear. She looked like a ramp model to me. Slim, tall, and beautiful. She was simple, yet she looked desperately pretty. As she came close, she looked at me for an instant and gave me a shy smile. I smiled. The next moment, she was walking towards the college gate. She did not even stop to talk to me. I then realized that two more girls were with her. I hadn't observed them. I knew they would be going to the café nearby. I stood there looking at her until she turned at the end of the street. I started by bike and went in the opposite direction. The road would circle around the campus, and that would give me another chance to look at her again. I quickly passed by the eatery and juice shop, but she wasn't there. She must have hurried her way into the café. I went around a couple of more times. Then I called to ask her to meet me outside the café. She did not answer my call. I tried again, and she disconnected my call. In a moment, she messaged me. 'Hey, I am with my friends now. I will call you later.' 'Okay,' I replied.

I knew that it would be close to another hour before she would come out. I went to the tea shop. Felix, Sam, and Vachan were already there.

'Aakash, what is up with you today? You were going around the college several times on your bike. Who are you looking for?' asked Felix.

'Hey, did you find someone pretty on the way?' asked Vachan.

'No, guys, nothing like that. I was just looking for my friend from the other department. He was supposed to meet me now, but I don't see him anywhere,' I said. I did not want to tell anybody about Aasma now.

I spent some time with them. Everybody went back to college. I told them that I had work and would not be attending the next class. I went and parked outside the café. I called her to check if she was still there and if she had a chance to meet me without her friends. She disconnected the call and messaged me that she was in class and would call later in the night.

I went home early that day. I was happy enough from seeing her for one day. I could always keep meeting her from now on. I was, in fact, surprised to see that she already had friends. Second day of college, and she was going out with friends already. That was quick.

***

She called me late in the night. I was awake, watching TV. I knew that she would be calling me.

'Hey, Aasma,' I said.

'Hey, Aakash.'

'You were looking pretty today,' I said.

'You were posing like a hero on your bike,' she said.

'Why didn't you meet me today? I wanted to talk to you. I was waiting for you. Outside the café,' I said.

'My friends were there with me. I don't want anybody to know about us so soon in college. That's why I didn't talk to you today,' she said.

'Why is that? What is the problem in it? Sooner or later they will get to know,' I said.

'No, Aakash, I don't want anybody in college to know this. If my aunt gets to know, then it will be a big trouble for me,' she said.

'Alright.'

'At least in the beginning we will be like that, then we can meet up later on,' she said.

Our conversation continued about the college, the campus, and so on for a while. We both had to wake up early for college the next day.

***

I now felt a completely different kind of excitement to go to college every day. I dressed up well every day. Every day she would smile at me and then disappear. Just for that one moment of eye contact and smile, I would miss classes and wait near the college entrance or the café. Back home, every night, we would talk about what happened with each other the whole day. This went on for about a month or so. In the meantime she was quickly making new friends. She had a group of friends in college by now.

One day, while I was in the computer lab, which we had twice in a week in the early evening hours, she messaged me. 'Aakash, can you meet me today?'

'What happened? Is there anything urgent?' I asked.

'Nothing. Just felt like talking to you. That's it,' she replied.

Wow! I thought. *She is asking me to meet up in college.* She told me the time. I replied that I would meet her right after I finished my class.

An hour later, the computer lab finished. I told Sam that I would be going home late and I wouldn't be able to drop him. I hurried to the parking lot, took my bike, and left the college. I didn't want Sam to see me and Aasma together anywhere near the college. I did not want everybody to know about it yet.

***

Aasma had messaged me that she would be waiting in the café and I should call her once I was done with my classes. I called her; she said that she would be going to the bus stop and asked me to meet her there. As I approached the bus stop, she crossed to the other side of the road and walked a few paces. The road that led to the bus stop was deserted. It was quite awkward standing in the middle of deserted road and talking to her.

'You're looking good today,' I said.

'Thanks. How was your day? Finished all your classes?' she asked.

'Yup, finished with all the classes,' I said.

'Do you really attend classes properly or do you just roam around the campus in your bike?' she asked. I just smiled.

'So do you have plans now?' she asked in a flirtatious tone.

I felt that she wanted to spend some time with me. Guess she wanted to go out, or had she already planned something for me?

'No plans now. I am not doing anything. Why?' I asked.

'Just asked,' she said.

Our conversation turned to everyday college happenings. I was waiting for her to ask me out. A while later, she said that she was getting late and that her aunt would be waiting for her. She would call me late at night.

***

This went on for another three weeks. No meeting in college. She only smiled if she saw me in campus. Late in the evening after all the classes, we used to meet up in the same street, talk for a while. Every night we slept late. I don't remember what we used to talk about over the call. Not sure how we used to get any topic to talk about. Guess we just wanted to hear each other's voice every night. It had become a routine for me. Sleep late, wake up late, and miss the first class. Along with me, Sam would also miss the first class. Every morning we would go to college late, Sam would go to meet up his girl friends, and I would head to the tea shop. Attend all classes or most of them. In the evening I met Aasma, spoke for a while, and headed back home. Late in the evening, I and Sam would meet up again in our usual hang-out place. Felix and Vachan also joined us often.

CHAPTER 10

It had been a month since Aasma had joined our college. One evening when I was with my usual group of friends yapping our time away, the topic of the new girl in college came up. Sam, as usual, was the first one to comment.

'Hey, did you guys see the new girl in the architecture department? I think she has joined recently. She is really good-looking. One of the best in our college,' Sam said.

'Yeah, I saw her. She doesn't speak much, I think. I have seen her a few times in the campus,' said Vachan.

'I have to find out more about her. I must find out her name first,' Sam said.

I did not get into this conversation. I knew who they were talking about. And I also knew that if they got to know her name, surely they would question me. They would certainly ask me if I knew her and if she was the girl whom I met in Mangalore. I chose to stay quiet. I knew that they would find out soon, and I would have to answer them. *When the time comes, I will answer them.*

***

A week later, Sam called me in the evening and asked me to urgently meet up in the usual place. He told me that

Felix and Vachan were already there. *Well*, I thought, *what is so urgent?* When I met them, the mood was not quite so urgent. 'Hey, Aakash is here. Welcome, Aakash!' Vachan said. The rest joined in welcoming me. I had no clue what was happening.

'Hey, guys, Aakash is going to buy us a drink,' Felix said.

'Why, boys, what is so special? Why am I buying you drinks?' I asked.

'Hey, tell me, what happened to the girl you met in Mangalore? No news about her lately?' asked Sam.

I knew that Sam had got to know that Aasma was the Mangalore girl who was now in our college. I did not expect this to be out so soon. And I would be caught if I tried to lie to them.

'The new girl that you guys were talking about the other day, she is Aasma. And yes, she is the girl I met in Mangalore,' I said.

Everybody started throwing questions on me together. They wanted to know everything that happened and why I did not tell them. Why did I keep it a secret?

'Guys, look, I should have told you this earlier. But I thought of telling you once things had settled down. I didn't mean to hurt you guys. Yes, this is the girl that I met in Mangalore. We were not in touch for a long time. I thought things had ended there. That is why I did not tell you. A few months ago, I started talking to Aasma again and this kick-started it off,' I said.

'You know I always thought I had seen that girl somewhere. She looked familiar to me. I have seen her photo online long back. Now I remember,' Sam said.

'And please don't tell this to anybody in college. I do not want this to spread. I like to see if things will really work out between us. You will certainly get to meet Aasma sometime soon,' I said.

'Alright, but next time don't keep secrets from us. We are your friends,' said Vachan.

'Yeah, I know. I am sorry, guys,' I said.

'Okay, order a drink for us now. That's your punishment for not telling us!' Felix shouted.

I returned soon after that. I thought of calling Aasma a little sooner and sleeping early. I was a little tired. She answered before even the first ring ended.

'Hey, Aakash, guess what. I was thinking about you now. I wanted to tell you something,' she said in a lovely tone.

'Yeah? What is that?' I asked.

'You know, one of my childhood friends is my classmate here. I met him after a long time. We studied together in school,' she said. 'I did not even know that he lived in Mysore.' She seemed happy about it.

'Good, I see you have already made quite some friends in college,' I said.

'Yup, and you know what, he was behind me in school. He used to like me back then.' She giggled.

'Yeah? What's his name?' I asked.

'Rishab. He lives near our college,' she said.

***

I was a little curious to know who the guy was. I asked Sam the next day if he knew anybody by that name in our college.

'Yes, I know him, why are you asking?' Sam said.

'Nothing. Just enquiring. Heard his name,' I said.

'He is Nayan's younger brother,' he said.

***

Nayan was one of the troublesome guys in the college. The only thing he did well was start a fight and beat up anybody who happened to cross him. I had seen people getting beaten up by Nayan and his friends many times outside the college campus.

The younger brother wasn't too far behind. He was also following the same thing as his brother. More seen outside the campus than in. Average height, scary looking, coloured hair and earrings. He looked like a typical street punk.

I was not happy that Nayan's younger brother was Aasma's friend. I did not like it at all. I did not want Aasma to even talk to Rishab. Moreover, she had told me that Rishab used to like her when they studied together in school. I just wanted Aasma as far away from him as possible. But how would I tell this to her? I could not tell it candidly. She may not feel good about it. She might feel that I was being possessive or I did not like her talking to guys. That was not my intention. I did not mind her talking to anybody other than the madman Rishab. But I could not hold it back. I had to tell her to keep her away from Rishab. I would have to tell her about him. He may have been a good guy in school but he was not anymore. I had to make her understand. But I did not know how to tell her. I would have to think of a way to tell this to her in a polite way.

***

While going to college, I asked Sam if he knew Rishab personally. He said that he had known him personally for a long time. They were from the same community. But he did not like Rishab either. He told me that many guys in our college were already trying for Aasma. She was one of the best-looking girls in the college. I thought of leaving the matter at that. It was not the best time to tell Aasma about Rishab. It might just be that old friends had met, and being classmates, it may have been a casual greeting. I knew that Aasma wouldn't be interested, but I did not trust Rishab. I knew how he was when it came to girls.

***

Since Aasma and I got together again, I had no interest in anything other than caring for her. I wasn't going out with my family, not attending any events and such. My whole day would be spent either thinking about her or talking to her. Even when I was with friends every evening in our hang-out place, I would be busy over the phone talking to her. Hour after hour would pass, but I never had enough of talking to her.

Simple things like having dinner along with my family were not happening anymore. I wouldn't have time to speak to my parents. My sister who was living in Bangalore had stopped calling me. Every time she called, my phone would be busy. I would feel irritated when my parents wanted me to go along with them to any social event. I didn't want to do any of that because I wouldn't have time to talk to her. As the days passed, the hours I spent on the phone were growing. After college, I would come home and spend time either online on social networking or talking to Aasma.

Nothing else had my interest anymore. No more watching TV or reading or painting. I was spending more and more time alone in my room. I just didn't want to be disturbed. Every night, my parents used to call me to have dinner along with them. That also bothered me. I would say that I'd join, then I would say that I'd have it later, and sometimes I would scream at my parents to stop calling me for dinner. I had lost sense of time. By the time I had finished talking to her every night, my parents would have long slept. Dinner would have become cold. I wasn't interested in having dinner even when my mom had prepared some of my favourite dishes.

My lifestyle had changed drastically. No family, less friends. At one point in time, I had lost touch with my family members. Rarely did I speak to my sister. Many things might have happened in the circle of my family and friends and I wouldn't have known. It was as if I was living in a shell, disconnected from the outside world. Mom would have bought new furniture, Dad planned to buy a new car, and I wouldn't have known about this. I had not attended many social gatherings that I was supposed to. People thought I was lost somewhere.

My parents did try to ask me about what was happening to me. They were quite concerned why I was acting unusually and why I was spending so much time alone in my room. I think they knew that every day I was talking to a girl. I guess they had given up on me. They had accepted my new way of life.

***

The increasing phone bill was coming hard on my daily allowance. Adding to that, I was buying new clothes very often, and all these needed money. Every day, I asked my dad for more money. I gave a dumb reason for the extra fuel and phone bill. Am not sure what had happened, but Dad never asked me anything about my increasing need for money. It was like he was happy to give me anything that I asked for. I wasn't feeling good about this, though. I didn't want to lie to my parents, but then again, it was the need of the hour. I wanted money.

An idea popped. I thought, *I'll ask my sister for monthly allowance.* She was working, so it would not matter to her. But I had to give her a reason. I had to convince her.

***

So I had the money I needed now. Phone bill was taken care of, fuel no problem. I was happy again. Aasma called me in the morning when I was about to leave for college. She told me that she didn't have the morning class and wanted to meet me. I asked her to meet me near the café.

We were in the café for quite a while. We both missed two of the morning classes. This became an everyday thing for us. Meet up in the café every morning, spent time chit-chatting.

As days passed, we wanted to spend more and more time together. The café wasn't the right place for it. How long could we drink and eat in the café? We needed a quieter place.

A few months later, we had enough of the café. A couple of paces down the street, there was a two-story run-down building. It used to be a printing press, it seems, as the board said. It looked like any activity was long shut down. People hardly noticed the building. The stairs leading to the upper floor seemed like the perfect place we were looking for. It was rarely used and was cosy enough for people looking for a quiet place in the midst of the urban buzz. The stairs were not wide but just enough for two people to sit comfortably. We couldn't be seen from the street as well. So this was our new hideout.

Flirtation between us had increased. Playful teasing, questions, feigned disinterest, the hair flick, and prolonged eye contact. Slowly but surely, these led to close proximity and brief touching. I loved the way she reacted. A tickle turned into a cuddle. An embrace ended up in a peck on the cheek. Every day it was growing—hot romance. Every minute of it was romantic. It was the best I could have asked for. Best days of my life yet.

***

Meanwhile my friends were growing more and more curious. I spent less time with them and the rest with Aasma.

'What do you do sitting there? What do you talk about the whole day long?' Felix asked when I met him in the evening.

'When are you going to introduce her to us?' Sam asked.

I told them to meet up the next morning in the café. I introduced Aasma to everybody. It was kind of a formal introduction. They had seen each other in the college campus. I had also told them about each other. Sam, being ever curious about girls, threw a few more questions at her. It was good to see Aasma getting along well with my friends. The last thing I wanted was to lose my friends because of her.

CHAPTER 11

I was online on Orkut and browsing through the Internet about the latest news. I was curious to see what was happening in Aasma's profile. I noticed Sam in the mutual friends list. He had also messaged her. I was surprised. It had been just a week since I introduced Aasma to him.

'What, Sam, you have already sent Aasma a friend request. You have also started messaging, it seems?' I asked Sam about it.

'Did she tell you that? I merely sent her a friend request. She accepted, and we were chatting for a while. Why? Shouldn't I do that?'

'Nothing as such. I just asked. Feel free,' I said.

From then on I and Aasma got together with my friends every day in the café whenever we had free time. I was happy that I had my friends with me and Aasma too.

Aasma asked me for Felix's and Vachan's phone numbers when we were in our hideout. She said she might need them just in case I was not reachable. I told her that they were my trusted friends and would be watching her back at a call's notice. I gave her the number. She said that she already had Sam's number. He had given it to her while they were chatting online.

***

Aasma didn't have as many classes one day, and she wanted to go out for a drive with me. I thought it'd be a good change for both of us. I agreed, but then I didn't have money. I didn't know where she wanted to go or what she wanted to do. I needed money, and so I thought I could borrow some from Vachan. He was a guy who always had money secretly stashed in his pocket. I met Vachan on the way to college. Aasma was waiting for me in the usual place. She had no classes until late afternoon and wanted to go somewhere quiet. We decided the best place was the riverside. It was about an hour's drive.

***

With lean traffic for most part of the drive, in an hour we reached a one-of-its-kind island-like backwater resort. For anybody looking for a break from the stress and strain of urban life, this was the place. I parked my bike. The cruise was ready to ferry us from the entrance on the roadside to the resort proper. Ten-minute chugging on the still waters with scenic beauty all round, skies dotted with bird formations, the chirping of birds and only nature for company, tucked away amidst still backwaters of the river, surrounded by a still-unpolluted natural environment was this wonderful riverside resort. It had a lot of open space and a walking avenue.

The lunch was amazing. After lunch, we spent time walking around the area. The walking avenue was overshadowed by huge trees, and every few meters, wooden benches were placed. The birds, the sunshine, the squirrels, and the smell of the sap. It's lovely; when you live in a city, you forget such things exist. Within those walls of bark, it's me, Aasma, and the amazing natural wildlife. We didn't speak as we walked, savouring the silence that nature served.

My leg started aching a little while later. I leaned back on a huge tree along the way. Aasma came close to me. I held her by the small of her waist. After months of flirtation, cuddling, and pecks, I was comfortable embracing her. But today she didn't stop there. She inched closer, smiling from an angle, and eyebrows raised; there was a flirtatious glitter in her eyes. Even though I was used to her close proximity, she was pushing it to a new level. In a slow meditative movement, she stretched her arms around my neck and leaned into me. This was not a peck on the cheek; I knew it was about to go beyond. I was pinned against the tree, and tipping in, she let her body rest on me. The softness of her body against my chest gave me a rush. We were millimetres apart. No room for air between our bodies, I dropped my neck to her side, the edge of my nose caressing her cheek along. I breathed slow and deep. I could smell her hair. The fresh aroma was intoxicating. I kissed her cheek. I kissed again and held it a bit longer. The next one closer to her lips. I stopped there. 'Don't you want to kiss on my lips?' she whispered into my ears. I didn't miss it. It was the first time we really kissed. It was unlike any other rush I had felt. We held the kiss long enough. It was intense. I kissed her again. It was filled with all the passion that we could muster. When we were finished, she opened her eyes, and there was a fresh twinkle in her eyes. I knew for certain that she liked it.

Starting from welcoming us to bidding farewell, every little detail was taken care of by the courteous staff. It was an excellent place to spend your day in peace. We spent much more time than we intended to. We didn't realize that we had spent hours. We returned later in the evening. Aasma really liked the place. She wanted to go again even before we had reached college. We would certainly visit the place again. I liked the way we spent the day. I wished every day to be like that.

I couldn't sleep that night. All I could do was recall the events of the day. Only the special moment was running through my mind. Surely she was mine now.

CHAPTER 12

Aasma was growing popular in college day by day. She had more and more friends in college now, unlike me. I liked to have fewer friends but lasting and trustworthy ones. Her chatting with Sam had become very frequent. He had told her many things about the college and the happenings of the college. I wasn't aware that people in our college had somehow gotten to know about me and Aasma. When I heard about it, I actually felt proud to have her with me. One of the most sought-after girls in college was with me. Aasma was also getting much attention from the guys, and I liked that. I had something that other guys couldn't have, and I took pride in that. You know the male ego.

Vachan was kind enough to lend me money whenever I needed. I don't even remember how much he had given me and how much I had returned. He never kept count of it. I think that is the best part about a friend. On every occasion I went out with Aasma, I had much-needed money to spend. I didn't have to plan another fake tuition fee from my dad. I and Aasma had been out to almost all possible places around Mysore.

***

I happened to check her profile online, and I saw that many boys from our college were on her friends list. She was also quite active in social networking, unlike me again. I was, as well, on the receiving end of unnecessary attention and scary looks from the guys, which I hated the most. It was a high time in my life. I had the most beautiful girl, attention, money, and time. Well, not to mention my academics were taking a big hit these days. But that didn't matter as long as I had the rest of the things.

In the meantime, my results weren't looking good either. I had failed in several subjects. I was also getting unnecessary attention from the college lecturers. My parents were called up one day to meet the principal about my attendance. Mom and Dad had met the principal. Dad never questioned me why I was not attending college. He walked into my room one day and said, 'Son, I understand this is the age where you explore and learn a lot. But I realize you're not heading in the right direction, and if this continues, you are certainly not going to complete your graduation. I hope you know what you are doing. If you need anything, just tell me. I am here for you.' I didn't have any answer for my dad. I think what my father said was right. I was not heading in the right way. But then again, I wasn't bothered about it much. Many of my friends who regularly attended classes had also failed in the examinations. It didn't mean that attending classes would magically pass me. I knew that I could clear my examinations later on.

The situation at home was also not appearing good. I had almost cut off any kind of interaction with my neighbours and distant relatives. I rarely had a talk with my parents. The shell I was living in was my world.

***

Sam called me in the morning. He wanted to meet me urgently. I was wondering what could be so urgent. He was waiting for me near the college entrance. Aasma was attending classes that time, so I didn't have anything important to do.

'Come, let's go have coffee. I want to talk to you about something important,' Sam said when I met him.

'Did you meet Aasma yesterday?' he asked as we sat in the café.

'Yeah, why?'

'Listen, don't take me the wrong way when I ask this. Are you really serious about your relationship with Aasma?'

'Of course, dude. Have you seen me interested in any girl other than her? Crushes are different. This is something else. Things between us are getting serious little by little. Anyways, tell me. What made you ask this? Do you think I am not serious about this relationship?'

'No, no. That is not what I meant. I do understand that you are very serious. I see that you are less interested in anything else apart from her. But recently I've been hearing talk about you two. And after what you said now, it's not looking good.'

'What do you want to say, Sam? I don't understand. You know how I am. Keep it straight,' I said apprehensively.

'Yes, I've known you for quite a long time now. But still I am not sure how to say it. It's difficult for me too.'

'Just say it,' I snarled.

He continued to say, 'A couple of weeks ago, I met Aasma's friends. You know the two girls who are always with her in college. I was talking to them, and your matter came up. They tell me that Aasma is not serious about you. It seems Aasma had told them herself. She claims that she can get a hundred guys like you if she wants. Moreover, they say that you are the one who is mad about her even though she is not very interested. They also told me that she has started to like Rishab.'

'Look, Sam, don't give me this crap. People talk all nonsense. I know Aasma very well, and I know how serious she is,' I said, annoyed.

'Do you think I am kidding you? Come on, Aakash, don't you believe me?' he said.

'No, I don't believe in what everybody is saying. I know about her well.'

'Okay, I've told you what I wanted to,' he said resignedly.

I knew he didn't like the way I took his words. I could see his expression.

'Thanks, but don't worry. Everything is fine,' I said to ease things off.

'No, Aakash, it's not fine!' he shouted. 'Even I felt the same. I did not believe it when the girls told me. I know some people try to feed you nonsense. But I also heard this from one of my friends. He is also in the same class as Aasma. He too told me the same thing. And it seems like Rishab and Aasma are getting a lot closer these days. People have seen them together in campus. You know what I mean.'

I did not respond. What he was saying was something I couldn't accept. I hated the fellow Rishab. Only I knew that Aasma and Rishab were schoolmates.

'I couldn't believe what I was hearing,' Sam continued. 'So I met Aasma yesterday. And you know what, she did something I couldn't have expected from her at all. She was straight in telling me that she didn't love you and she is not interested in you. She told me the same thing that her friends had told me earlier. I asked about Rishab. She says that he is her good friend and that they were schoolmates.

'And she says that you are one who is mad about her,' he said. 'I could not take this. I told her that she is the one who wants you and is mad about you. She said she can prove it. "If you want, I can prove it. I will not call or message him from today. See how he wants me. Even he is not as serious, and I know that," Aasma told me.'

I could not take this anymore. Whatever Sam was telling me made sense. It made sense under the circumstances. Aasma had not called me that morning. Every morning, we met. But today she did not even message me.

I called her. She disconnected. I called twice again, and the call was disconnected. I looked up at Sam and said, 'She must be in class.'

'No, dude, they don't have class now. I met her friends this morning in campus,' he said.

I messaged her, but there was no response for a long time. I finished my coffee in silence. Sam also fell quiet. I was upset by this news. What I was feeling was something I had never felt before. I felt betrayed.

I couldn't just sit there quietly. I was losing my patience. I called Aasma again, but it went unanswered. Sam got a message. He passed me his phone. It was a message from Aasma.

'Why is he calling me?'

I was so angry that I wanted to throw the phone or break anything around that I possibly could. I asked Sam not to respond.

I did not call her after that, and neither did she. Nor did she reply when I messaged her a couple of days later. My calls were not answered; my messages were not replied to. I had almost stopped attending college. I spent my day in the café or the tea shop or roaming around the campus hoping to see Aasma.

I really wanted to see her and ask for myself if it was true. I wanted to see how she'd react. I wanted to see the look on her face when she said that.

***

Two weeks later, I saw her walking towards the ice cream parlour with her friends. I stopped my bike on the other side of the road to look at her. She looked at me. Her expression told me everything I wanted to know. I had my answers. She didn't even flinch when she saw me. It was as if I was not there at all. She was laughing and giggling with her friends, and here I was, hurt to the core, and she had no expression whatsoever. I stood there on my bike for a long time. I had this mounting anger. To my disbelief, I saw Rishab come up and park his bike. I saw him going into the ice cream parlour. My anger had reached new heights. I could not believe what I was witnessing.

Just a week ago, she wanted to go out with me and kissed me and promised the whole world. And a week later, she was acting as if she had never known me. And why on earth did she want to be with Rishab?

This was too much for me to accept. I could hardly believe how people could change in a matter of days. So heartless.

***

I stopped going to college. I'd sit awake for most of the night. Every now and then I checked my phone for any call or message. I even started smoking along with my friends. The rest of the day I spent in a tea shop smoking my life away. I'd run to my phone every time it beeped. Since the time I had Aasma in my life, people called me less and less; I was talking to Aasma more and more. I did not receive as many calls other than from Aasma. Either it'd be from my close friends or Aasma. Nobody else called me. Every time my phone made a noise, I helplessly hoped it was her message or call. And to my increasing disappointment, it seemed like she was not going to try and contact me.

My parents had also not asked me why I was not attending college. It was an addition to my already depressed mind. My parents had also stopped caring about me. I lived like a stranger in my own house. It had been a month since I last focused on college. Most of the time I'd be sleeping, smoking, or imagining what she might be doing. I imagined her to be laughing and flirting with Rishab. I imagined them together in the café, and the image was not easy on my now-depressed state.

***

My phone beeped. I had now stopped jolting at every sound of my phone. In fact, I wanted to be as far away from my phone as possible. I didn't even remember where I had kept my phone.

I was about to sleep after lunch when I checked my phone. There was a message from Aasma. I opened it anxiously.

It read 'Meet me in the evening. Want to talk.'

I checked the time. I still had two hours to go. I couldn't hold on to my anxiety. I quickly dressed up. I thought I could wait in the café. I didn't want to waste time travelling in the midday traffic. I wanted to be somewhere in the vicinity so that I could meet her as soon as she called.

I was juggling my feelings. I imagined her apologizing for what she had done. I also imagined her walking up to me and saying that she didn't love me anymore, or what if she brought Rishab with her and said, 'Here is the guy I love'? And I imagined how I should be reacting to all this. I was desperately hoping that she'd say sorry, that nothing had happened between us and that she still loved me.

I met her in the usual place when she called me. She looked miserable. The charm in her was lost.

'Hey,' I said as she approached.

'Hey.'

'How are you?'

'Fine,' she said. 'Aakash, I want to ask you something, and please tell me the truth,' she said in an unhappy tone.

'What?'

'Do you really love me or not? Sam told me that you do not love me and that you are not interested in me. Please tell me right away, and I will not trouble you anymore.'

'What? When did he tell you all this?' I asked, feeling annoyed.

'Doesn't matter. Now answer me please. That's why I stopped messaging or calling you.'

'Wait, Sam must have been kidding with you,' I said.

She stared across the street. No noticeable reaction to what I had said.

'Please believe me, Aasma. I do love you. He must have been kidding, and you have taken it seriously,' I said in defence.

It took me another hour or so of convincing to finally make her believe that I really loved her and what Sam had said was crap. Now I clearly understood what had created the trouble. It was Sam. But what I did not understand was why. Why did he do it? Why did he do such a thing as to try taking us apart? I didn't think he was kidding when he told me about Aasma. What were his intentions behind this? I actually wanted to ask Sam right away. But us being close friends for so long, I did not know how to ask him. I called up Vachan and Felix to the café to talk about it.

***

Felix and Vachan looked on as I told them about the recent events. They too had the same question. Why did he do that?

'You know how he is when the matter is about girls. Maybe he is just jealous,' Felix said.

'Maybe, but we trusted him. Let's just go ask him upfront. I think he is in the movies with college girls. It's about to finish in half an hour. We'll talk to him there,' Vachan said.

Sam walked up to us when he saw us waiting outside.

'Hey, guys, what are you doing here?' he asked, seemingly excited.

'Sam, did you tell Aasma that I don't love her and I am playing with her?' I asked angrily.

He was taken aback by the question. I think he had not expected that we would come to know about this clever act.

'What? No. Why would I say that? Did she tell you? Have you started believing in girls more than your friends?'

I didn't want to drag the matter further. Even if he denied it, his response had been clear. I knew he was the culprit.

If I pushed this subject, he would certainly create a bigger misunderstanding between us later on. I thought it was better to let go of the issue. At least, our friendship would remain.

I know Sam had played a clever game. I told Aasma about it later that night. We decided not to believe him if he said any such thing again. I was glad that the mix-up was resolved between me and Aasma. Things came back to normal again. We met every morning in the same place as earlier.

But somewhere at the back of my mind, I did not forget the moment I saw Aasma and Rishab. I and Sam had been friends for a long time. We had been through many things. He was one of the most trusted guys on my list. Had he been telling the truth? Maybe, maybe not.

Chapter 13

I and Aasma both needed a break from all the recent events. We wanted to get away for a while from all the mess around. We just wanted to be left alone, be together, cuddle up, and rekindle the romance between us. Moreover, it had been long since we had been out together.

We were in one of the beautiful resorts around Mysore. As though she had sensed her presence in my thoughts, Aasma appeared behind me, wrapping her long arms around my bare shoulders. I stared at her in the mirror's surface as her fingers traced my jawline. I splashed water on my face and turned to face her. She was wearing a short skirt and a tank top. She looked fabulous. Stood on her toes and kissed me.

'Don't rub the lamp if you don't want the genie to come out,' I said in a joking manner.

'Maybe the genie should come out,' she replied.

I was no longer sure if she was joking or not. All I knew was that I had a serious stiff. I think this must have excited Aasma. That obviously worked out; before you knew it, we were walking towards the bed. It started out innocently enough; I never thought it would go as far as it did. She stopped before we reached the bed. She put me up against the wall and told me to close my eyes. I cheated and only squinted. She leaned up to whisper in my ear, pressing soft against my chest. I could feel her even through her tank top.

'I want you,' she whispered. And we kissed.

We had been kissing for a while now. She began to breathe more heavily.

'I really want to feel you,' she said and then took off her tank top.

By now I was scared. I was absolutely turned on, but I had no idea what to do. So I did the most natural thing. I took off my shirt. From this moment on, I knew that she would have the final say in what was going to occur for the rest of the evening, and that is exactly what happened.

We were both nervous about this. I gently pushed her towards the bed. She lay down, and we started exploring each other. I remember the smoky room almost like a cloud with a dim yellow light. She took it herself and guided me inside her. The warm and moist sensation was phenomenal. Eventually I remember lying on my back after making love to her. I don't how long it lasted; that is where my memory is unclear.

The next morning, on the way back, we didn't really talk. I feared I might have made the biggest mistake of my life. Needless to say, I was disappointed with the whole experience. I guess I also had high expectations. I thought the whole experience would have been more like what we see in television or the big screen—smooth, passionate, and stress-free lovemaking. But later I realized that it was normal for me to act in such a way. It's natural to feel some stress when making love; it was all a new experience for me. I was quite happy for 'growing up' in a way.

***

Aasma was growing ever more popular in college. Her friendship with Rishab was also growing little by little, and this concerned me. I had tried to tell her about him one day, but she wasn't ready to hear any more about him. He was good to her, and he was her friend. That is all that mattered to her. Our conversation had turned into an argument, but I had made it very clear to her that I did not like that person and I did not want her to have any kind of connection with him. Of course, the answer from her was a forthright no and that she would talk to him if he talked. If not, she would not try to make contact with him. But if he did, she could not refuse it. Finally, I had to give up when she said that she had known Rishab even before me.

She said that she loved me but she would always be Rishab's friend. Just because I didn't like him, she would not stop talking to him.

'If I don't like your friends, will you stop talking to them? Then how can you expect the same from me?' she had said.

I thought it was best to leave it at that. I didn't want to continue further. But I was disappointed that she was supporting him in any capacity.

***

More often than not, I could link Rishab to anything that happened between us. I hated that guy to the core, and she did not like the fact. We often ended up in a fight whenever the topic was about Rishab. This was coming hard on our relationship. I had actually seen them together in campus one day. I did not understand if she was intentionally doing this, which was kind of a signal to me that she would continue to do so no matter what and I had no control over it. Certainly things weren't right when the subject was about Rishab.

But besides the often troubling subject, our relationship was going well. We spent good time with each other talking, and we waited at the slightest opportunity to go out for a ride or cuddle wherever we found cosy and share intimate moments. That wasn't enough; our nightly calls lasted longer than ever these days. Good thing that my sister was kind enough to keep sending me money from time to time. I had pulled off one more fake tuition fee from my dad when I was low on cash, and I had to return money to Vachan. My debt was increasing, my phone bill was mounting, and I spent even less time doing anything else other than being occupied with Aasma. Still, I was the happiest person.

***

Surprisingly her number was busy when I called late at night, which was unusual. She returned my call after a while.

'Hey, you were busy. Whom were you talking to at this hour?' I asked.

'I was talking to Saloni. She had trouble with her boyfriend. I had to talk her out of it. It took me almost an hour,' she replied giggling.

Saloni was one of her close friends in college. She was always into one or the other kind of relationship.

It really started to annoy me when Aasma's phone was busy late nights.

'Oh, Saloni again. I don't know when she is going to get over her love stories. It is sometimes irritating,' Aasma said.

'Then why don't you tell her not to call you?' I said.

'How can I say that, Aakash? She is my friend,' she replied.

***

Saloni had become a regular disturbance during our late-night calls. I actually started to hate her for that. Even when I was speaking to Aasma, in the silence of the night, I could hear the 'call waiting' beep of Aasma's phone. Saloni would be calling her late into the night. At times, I asked Aasma to call her back and tell her that she would speak to her in the college next morning. It was a regular interruption for us. If not for calls, Saloni would be messaging Aasma. Every time Aasma checked her messages, our conversation would be interrupted. The barter of messages would continue until Aasma responded to her. I could hear the noise of keys as frantic Aasma replied to her message. I was irritated big time with this pause.

Several times I was so upset with the constant interruption that I told Aasma I would not be calling her if Saloni continued troubling us. And to my surprise, Aasma never asked Saloni not to disturb her during the nights.

'I cannot ask her not to call me. She is one of my best friends,' Aasma had said.

No surprise, the conversation ended in an argument.

***

This had started to occur regularly. I would be upset with Saloni's act, and Aasma was all right with it. Several times our late-night call was cut short just because of this. Sometimes I didn't even call Aasma at night. I just wanted her to get over Saloni and then call me when she had no disturbance. And every time this happened, Aasma would not call me or message me, let alone meet me the next day in college. At times this went on for two days in a row. Always I was the one to call her and apologize, only after which things would be normal between us.

***

In the recent weeks, I had noticed subtle changes in Aasma's activities. She was continuously occupied on the phone, messaging.

'My friends are messaging me from class. They also call me sometimes from class. It's thrilling for them to hide below the desk, call somebody, and talk while the lecture is going on,' she replied when I asked.

Can't believe what girls did these days. Whenever I and Aasma were out together, her friends kept texting her. This had become a nuisance for me. I wanted to spend time with her, and she would be fiddling with her phone. Several times she stepped away to answer their calls and talk to them for a while. She would be out of earshot, and no wonder—the girls would be talking in whispers. And I would be left alone, wondering what they might be talking about. Why couldn't they just listen to the lecture or not attend the class if they were not interested? Why disturb us?

'Saloni is calling me to attend the next class. It's important, it seems. I'll have to leave, Aakash,' Aasma left saying when her friends called up from class. Everything her friends did was now annoying me. Seems like they didn't want us to be together.

***

I noticed the new ring she was wearing. 'Hey, Aasma. Nice ring. When did you buy it?' I asked.

'It's a gift. My aunt bought it for me.'

She didn't sound excited to talk about her gift. Wonder why she did not bother to show me. I didn't try asking much about it though.

***

Again and again her number was busy when I called her. It was annoying to find Aasma talking to Saloni every night when we were supposed to be talking. I disconnected the call and started watching TV. She'd call me when she was done with Saloni.

'Sorry, Aakash, I kept you waiting.'

'No problem. I'm going to talk to Saloni about this. I don't like her doing this,' I said.

'Hey, my cousin called up. I was talking to him.'

'What cousin calls you up at this time?'

'He is crazy. He often calls me up late in the night. I usually don't receive his call. Today he called me thrice, so I spoke to him for a while,' she said.

'You really have some crazy set of people around you, Aasma. Your friends, your cousins,' I said.

'I know,' she giggled.

***

Her number was busy when I called her. She was supposed to meet me in the complex before the morning class. I waited for a while and called again. Still it was busy. Irritated, I sent her a message that I would meet her later and left to attend the morning class.

She called me in the afternoon.

'Hey, where are you?' I asked.

'Near my class. Where are you? Why didn't you answer my call? At least respond to my message.'

'What message? I didn't get any call or message from you,' she said.

That was strange. Why would she say that?

'Alright. I'll meet you later.' I hung up.

'What has happened to your phone?' I asked when I met her in the evening.

'Nothing. It's fine. Why?'

'Then why didn't you get my message or call?'

'Look, Aakash, how do I know? Did you even call me this morning?'

'Yes, twice. We were to meet up this morning.'

'Why would I lie to you? Check my phone if you want to. Oh, and sorry, I was late for the morning class so couldn't meet you. Must have been a network problem.'

'Okay, I'll talk to you later.'

At home I started to feel that things were not going right.

Unexpectedly, our call ended quite soon.

'Hey, darling.'

'Hey, what are you doing?'

'Nothing much. Hey, listen, my cousins have come home. I cannot talk to you today. My cousins will be there, and I don't want them to know anything about this.'

'Alright. Bye.'

'Love you. Bye.' She hung up.

That was different. She did sound excited. She had never called me darling yet. And neither had she said 'love you' before. It was really nice to hear that from her. I think it was the first time she said that to me. That was enough for me to lose my sleep all night. I was in my dream world dreaming about her. I wanted to see her when she said that. I was really looking forward to meeting her the next day. I felt excited. I wanted to talk to her again and listen to those words again. I called her again late at night. Her number was busy. I guessed she was busy talking to her cousins, so I wanted to trouble her. I kept calling her a few more times for the next half hour.

'Aakash, what happened? Why are you calling so many times? My cousins are here. I can't talk to you,' she messaged me.

'Nothing. I'll see you tomorrow,' I replied.

I didn't want to irritate her too much, so I stopped. Anyway, I would be meeting her the next morning. I let her enjoy with her cousins.

***

'Hey, why did you call me so many times last night?' she asked, sitting beside me in the stairs.

'Nothing, I wanted to irritate you.' I smiled.

She gave me a naughty stare when I said that. I hugged her and kissed her sorry.

'Next time you irritate me, I will not talk to you at all.'

'Okay, I won't.' I kissed her again. 'By the way, you know, you said "love you" just before you hung up the call yesterday.'

She blushed. 'I know. Shouldn't I say that? I do love you, Aakash.'

'No, no. It felt nice to hear it from you. You haven't said that at all.'

'Yes. If it makes you feel good, I'll say that to you every night.'

The rest of the day seemed like minutes for us. We didn't attend a class today. But it was nice being this way. It had been a long time since we spent the whole day together.

'Hey, how about a long ride tomorrow morning?' I asked when we were about to leave.

'Okay, cool. I'll see you tomorrow.'

'Love you,' she whispered.

Gosh, my heart went nuts. I watched her go. I wanted to hear it again and again and yet would never be satisfied. I had to wait for her call tonight.

***

I don't know what we spoke about, the night before. We spoke until 4 a.m. From college to people and lust to fashion. I guess Saloni called several times; I could hear the beeping noise, but it didn't bother me. I was in a good mood. We planned to ride out to a café that was around a two-hour drive from Mysore. In fact, I had wanted to take Aasma to that café for a long time.

It was quite late in the morning when I woke up. I was going to miss all classes today. I called up Aasma. She was in the college already. It surprised me. Did she not sleep yesterday? I dressed up, skipped breakfast, and left for college.

'Hey, Aakash, sorry, I won't be able to go out today. I have an important class to attend. Saloni tells me that many lecturers have noted my name. I have to attend. Please don't mind,' Aasma said when I met her in college.

'Come on, Aasma. Just once, can't you miss the class? You can attend all classes tomorrow,' I said.

'Sorry, darling, not this one. I don't want the principal to call my parents and complain. We'll plan up again. Sorry. I'll have to attend all classes regularly now. I'll talk to you later,' she said and left for her class.

I had been totally ready for the ride. I was all dressed up, had arranged money and the fuel needed. I was disappointed. Aasma left for class. I went to spend the day playing snooker.

Chapter 14

'Aasma, why haven't you been answering my calls lately?' I asked.

'Nothing, Aakash, I've been busy lately. I am attending all classes these days.'

'You don't even meet me as you did earlier. What is happening?'

'I know, Aakash, my friends say that I've been noted by the lecturers, and they might complain to my parents. So am just being careful. More over, internals and exams are fast approaching. I have to concentrate on that as well.'

'Yeah, right. But, Aasma, I keep missing you a lot.'

'I miss you too, Aakash. I'll call you after class.' She hung up.

Aasma and I hadn't been meeting up regularly. I felt that we had started to grow apart gradually. I was just scared that it might reach the point where we would not be able to stay together. I wasn't going to let that happen.

***

Sam called me in the evening. 'Hey, Aakash, where are you?' he asked.

'Home. Why? What is the matter?'

'Nothing, I thought you were in the shopping mall. I saw Aasma with a guy, thought you were also there.'

'No, I don't know about it. I am home.'

'Alright, I'll see you tomorrow.' He disconnected.

Well, what is Aasma doing in the shopping mall? She would have told me if she were going. Why didn't she tell me? I called Aasma to find out.

'Tell me, Aakash,' she answered.

'Hey, darling, what are you doing in the shopping mall?'

'Shopping obviously. How do you know that I am in the mall?'

'My friend saw you there. He told me.'

'Do you have friends everywhere?'

'Well, what can I say? I've been living in this city for a long time now. So I do have quite some friends,' I chuckled.

'Okay, with my aunt. I can't talk to you. I'll call you later.' She hung up.

***

'Hey, darling, done with your shopping?' I asked.

'Yup, bought a few clothes. What did you do today?'

'Nothing much. How much did you spend?'

'I don't know. My aunt paid.' She tittered.

'Who was the guy with you?'

'Which guy? Nobody was with me. I was with my aunt.'

'Yeah? My friend saw a guy with you it seems.'

'No, no. He must have seen somebody else,' she said.

'Alright, how about going out tomorrow?'

'Sorry, Aakash, I can't go out. I have important classes tomorrow.'

'Aasma, when will I get to meet you? You are really busy these days.'

I heard beeps again. She paused to check her phone. Guess Saloni was calling again.

'Is Saloni your girlfriend?' I laughed.

'Hey, I am not like that. I don't know why she keeps calling me. Crazy girl. Anyways, I'll talk to you later. Love you.' She hung up.

***

After the morning class, I and Sam went to the cafeteria. Sam wanted to meet somebody, and I didn't want to attend the next lecture. We were wandering in the college campus when I saw Saloni and her friend. I guess they didn't have class. I thought if they both were here, then Aasma would also be joining them. I dropped off Sam near the cafeteria. I spoke to Saloni and her friend for a while. They told they didn't have classes now. I asked if Aasma was going to join them here, and they were not sure about it. I thought of going out with Aasma if they didn't have classes now. I thought she could have called me if she had free time. It had been quite some time since we spent good time together. *I better call and tell her about my plans before she heads home.* I said bye to Saloni and left to call Aasma.

'Hey, Aasma, heard you don't have class now. I met Saloni here. Where are you?' I asked.

'I am near my class.'

'Listen, anyway you don't have class now. Shall we go out today?' I asked.

'No, Aakash, my friends have planned to go out for a movie in sometime.'

Saloni had not told me about this.

'Oh, I just met Saloni. She didn't tell me about this. So I thought of taking you out today.'

'No, Saloni is not coming. I am going with other classmates. I'll call you later,' she said.

Another chance missed. She seldom had free time, and still she decided to go to the movies instead of spending time with me. Another disappointment. I spent another three hours playing snooker. I was about to head home when I thought I might as well meet Aasma if she was back from the movies. I checked the time. By the time I reached there, she would be out from the movie. I was waiting outside the theatre. I had already tried calling her, but she had not answered. It was too crowded, and maybe she could not answer my call. People were rushing out the exit. I saw Rishab coming out. It really pissed me off. I should have thought about this. He was in the same class. I saw Aasma and her friends near the parking lot. She had left the theatre. I was wondering why she didn't answer my call. No chance of going out today again. I thought of asking her about this later.

***

'Why? Shouldn't he be in the same movie theatre as me? After all, we are in the same class and all my classmates had planned for a movie outing. I told you that earlier,' she said. She sounded really pissed off at me. I shouldn't have asked her. What she said was right. They were in the same class. Perhaps I was overreacting.

'Alright. Relax,' I said.

'Relax? You piss me off like this and then ask me to relax?'

'Okay. Am sorry.'

'Listen, Aakash, I don't know what you are thinking, but let me tell you, I did not talk to him. I did not know he was in the same movie. He must have come late.'

'Okay. I feel like punching his face every time I see him. Sorry I asked you.'

'If you hate him, it doesn't mean everybody should be doing the same!' she shouted.

'Okay. Leave it. I got it.' I hung up on her. I did not like the fact that she was taking his side. Maybe I had pissed her off. Maybe I was taking this little thing too seriously. Maybe I was being too possessive. I don't know.

***

'Sorry I hung up on you,' I said. 'I realized I was the one who had taken it to the next level. I shouldn't have made it a big thing and argued about it,' I said. I had overreacted. I knew that my questions had hurt her. I did not want her to feel that I did not like her going out with friends. I did not want to look like a possessive person, which I was not. Still, the way I spoke to her might have made her feel that way.

'What sorry?' She still sounded upset.

I did not answer her.

'See, Aakash, I know what you are thinking. But it is not that way.'

'What am I thinking?'

'I know you think that I was in the movie with him. That's why you asked me such questions. Maybe that is why you were there.'

'What? No. That is not what I think about you, Aasma. Why are you taking it the other way?' I said. Maybe she was right in a way. Somewhere in my mind, I did have this thought, that she was with him in the movie. Guess that made me react the way I did. As it turned out, my assumptions were completely wrong. And I had ticked her off. I was the reason she was upset.

'Whatever it is, Aakash, remember one thing. I can never lie to you, and I promise that I will never leave you.'

'I know, Aasma, why are you saying all this?'

I heard beeps again. Call waiting beep.

'My dad is calling. I'll talk to you later.' She hung up.

This was going in a different direction than I thought. Maybe she was right in a way but not entirely. I never felt that she was lying to me. I didn't feel that she was ever going to leave me. Now she thought that I felt she was with Rishab and that she was lying to me. She thought that I did not believe her. I called her after a while. Her phone was busy. I did not try again. I did not want to talk about all this when she was upset. Things would only get worse. I'd have to meet her in college and talk things through. I had little sleep that night.

**

'I know how you feel, Aakash. But what can I do if he is in the same movie as I am? We are in the same class. I can't tell him not to come.' She sounded like she was pleading now. She did look at me when she said it. She looked cute, by the way. She was doodling in her book. I just kept looking at her. Her sparkling earrings made me want her. I gently touched her earring.

'Don't touch me. You are such a bad person,' she said in a playful voice. I gently pulled her closer to me and kissed her.

'Don't ever do that to me, Aakash. I am not going to leave you,' she said, her voice low as she rested on my shoulders.

'I know, and I love you for that,' I whispered in her ear. I held her for a long time. I didn't want to let her go until I felt satisfied.

'I'll take you out sometime,' I said, caressing her face.

'Yeah. Let's go out sometime. I want to be with you.'

Chapter 15

'Aasma, I heard that you were with Rishab this morning,' I said, sounding pissed off. It upset me every time I heard his name.

'Yes. Who told you?'

'Someone told me. It doesn't matter. But you know I don't like you talking to him, let alone meeting him. Why did you meet him?' I was even more pissed off.

'He just wanted to talk to me. I can't run off if someone talks to me.'

'But why didn't you tell me? Why do you talk to him when I don't like you doing that?'

'Listen, Aakash, I cannot just turn away when somebody wants to talk to me. To tell you the truth, he cooks up stories about me if I don't talk to him. I know you don't like it, but what can I do? I don't want him to spread ill things about me, so I talk to him sometimes. I avoid it, but sometimes I have to talk to him.'

'Why does he do that?'

'I don't know. You can go ask him. You don't know all that he does in college. I just don't tell you all these things,' she said. 'He teases me in class if I avoid talking to him. He calls me names in class, and his gang of friends laughs at whatever he says. You will not understand what I am going through. You are only bothered about yourself.'

'Fine. I know how to take care of him. I will give him the right treatment.'

'Aakash, please don't do anything. I don't want things to get worse. If you talk to him, he will keep quiet, but when you are not around, he does that even more.'

'So what do you expect me to do? You don't want me to do anything about it?'

'Please do not do anything. I will solve it myself,' she said. 'I will talk to you later. I have to wake up early tomorrow. I have an important class. Love you.' She hung up.

Damn. What was it about girls? They tell us their problems, and they don't let us to do anything about it. Then why do they even tell us their problems if they want us to do nothing about it?

***

'We are going out for a group dinner. My classmates have planned for a dinner this evening,' she said when we were at the complex building.

'Will Rishab also be there?' I asked.

'Of course. Most of my classmates are coming.'

'Can you not go?' Again I did not like the idea that she would be in the same place as Rishab. I did not even want him anywhere near Aasma. The thought of him being in the same room as her upset me.

'How can I not go? My friends will feel bad if I don't go.'

What was she thinking? She knew that Rishab would be there. She knew I didn't like him. She also knew that he might trouble her, and yet she wanted to go. What was wrong with her?

'I hate him. I feel like punching him,' she said, seeming upset. 'I know he can't do anything to me. Let's see what happens. I guess I'll not be able to call you tonight. I may be tired after the dinner. I'll meet you tomorrow. I have to attend class now.'

***

'Why do you want to change your number again? You have already changed it thrice in the last few months,' I asked Aasma. She had already changed her number three times in the last few months. I didn't understand how some people could handle all the contacts and send the new number to all their contacts. Every now and then there would be additions of new tariffs, but what was the need to change number for the sake of ever-changing tariff plans? And every time she did that, she chose not to use the same service provider as mine. I had quite good tariff plans, which let me have twice as much talk time if the calls were within the same service provider. Even if she wanted to change her number, why not chose the same as mine and talk twice as much? I didn't know what sort of irresistible tariffs the other networks were offering.

***

'He messages me in class. Not just that, he sometimes calls me.'

I knew who she was referring to. Yet I wanted to hear it from her.

'Who?' I asked and waited for the expected answer.

'Rishab. He messages me when I am in class.'

'What message? What do you reply?'

'Just the usual casual messages. I try not to talk to him in class. So he messages. And if I don't reply to him, he starts calling me.'

'What, is he mad or what?' I asked angrily.

'I guess so. He says that he is crazy about me.'

'What did you reply?'

'What should I reply? I didn't reply to it, and he started calling me. I had to switch off my phone.'

I muttered about it. This guy was getting on my nerves now. What did he want?

'What does he want from you?'

'He just wants me to talk to him. I avoid him a lot. And if I do so, he starts his monkey business.'

'Did you tell him that you are not interested and that you have a boyfriend?'

'No, Aakash. I haven't told anybody about us apart from few close friends. I don't want him to spread rumours about us..'

'What rumours will he spread? Let him do whatever he wants. It doesn't matter to us.'

'It may not matter to you, Aakash, but it matters a lot to me. I'm a girl. I don't want anybody to talk ill about me. And he sometimes calls me in the night. I talk to you every night. He keeps calling again and again when my number is busy. I have asked Saloni to tell him not to call me but still he does,' she said.

***

'No, Aakash, I don't want you to compromise your attendance. We can go out some other time,' she said.

'You were the one who wanted to go out for a long time,' I said.

'Yes. But not today. We can go out some other time.'

I don't know from where these girls get their brains. Once in a while we get a chance to go out, and yet she is worried about my attendance.

***

'Hey, how does it look?' Aasma asked me excitedly. Her dad had bought her a new vehicle. For a long time she had been asking her dad for a two-wheeler, and finally it was here. She looked really happy. 'Do you like the colour?'

'Congrats, darling!' I said. 'Yes, I like the colour.'

It was a new model with the latest graphic stickers. It was one of the most popular mopeds amongst the college kids. I had seen it numerous times. Yet I felt happy for her. I was happy for one more thing: now that she had a vehicle, we could meet up whenever we want to, wherever we wanted. Happy me.

I took her new vehicle for a ride just so that she would feel happy about it. It is the usual thing to take it for a ride when somebody has got a new vehicle. Moreover, she wouldn't feel good if I didn't take it for a ride. She might think that I was not happy about it.

'You know what, I'm going to join tuitions very soon. I badly needed a vehicle. Every day I used to ask my dad to buy me one, and here it is today,' she said.

'What tuitions?' I asked. I don't remember her mentioning anything about tuitions.

'Yes, tuitions for some subjects that I feel are difficult. Three days a week.' She smiled. I think she was looking forward to the tuitions so that she could take her new vehicle out for a ride. Good for me again. Guess we could meet up after tuitions in the evening. I thought of asking her later on, or she might as well ask me to meet her after tuitions. I didn't want to come out looking all so ready for it. I wanted her to ask me that. So I considered waiting for it as the best thing to do now.

***

'Aasma, where were you this evening?' I asked when she called me in the night. Sam had told me that he had seen Aasma and Rishab together in the evening. I wanted to know if it was true. Sometimes you get to hear things that are not really true.

'I was out with my sister,' she said in an even tone as if nothing was unusual.

'Were you out with Rishab?'

'I was out with my sister. She wanted to go shopping. I happened to meet him in the shopping mall, and I spoke to him for a while.'

'Why do you still talk to him when you hate him? You don't like him, but you still stop to talk when you see him,' I said angrily.

'Then what should I do? Run away if I see him?'

I hung up on her.

Damn you, girl, I told myself. What can you say to that?

***

'I have class now. I cannot stay here all day long. Please let me go, Aakash. How long will you hold me?' she said playfully, elbowing out of my clasp and stepping away.

'Hey, come on,' I said, throwing my arms out.

'What? I have class now, Aakash. You also go and attend. Now come on,' she said, tugging me up.

'Do you have to attend this class? Can't we spend some more time here?' I said, holding her small waist.

She gave a peck on my cheek and said, 'I think that should do for now. Go attend class and let me also attend. Already my lecturers have noted my name. They've already sent a note to my aunt about my attendance.'

'What? When did that happen? You've been attending classes regularly now,' I said.

'Yes, now. I wasn't earlier,' she said with a wink. 'And you are the reason for it,' she said, making a kissy face.

Ohh, how could somebody resist that?

'How about meeting up this evening?' I asked.

'I have tuitions, darling.'

'Can't you skip tuitions?'

'No, darling. I cannot. I want to clear my exams.'

'How about after tuitions?'

'I don't go out in the evening, honey,' she said, elbowing me. 'And don't come near my tuitions. I won't even stop to talk to you. I'll go directly home after my tuitions. My aunt is keeping an eye on me. She has asked my tutor to keep watch as well.'

'What is your aunt? A spy?' I asked, trying to be funny.

'Yes, she is, kind of. And all because of you,' she said, hitting me on my chest.

'Wow. What did I do? If you skip your classes, not my problem,' I said.

'What? I skip classes so that I can be with you.' She elbowed me harder this time. 'Now let me go attend class.'

'So no meeting today?' I asked. I was a little disappointed. I was hoping that we could meet after tuitions. If that was easier, we could meet every day.

'No, darling. I'll meet you tomorrow in college.' She gave me another peck on my cheek and left. I had no other option but to go to my class.

Nowadays people had started to look at me as if I were an alien in my own class. I barely attended my classes. And the days I attended, everybody asked me what was special today that I thought of listening to the lecture; even the lecturers asked the same thing. It was odd to answer them. They all knew what I was up to when I was not in class.

***

'Where do you want to go today?' she asked. I had asked her if we could go out today at least, when I met her in the complex building.

'I don't know. The same place as last time perhaps. If you say yes, I'll have to arrange a few things,' I said.

'I don't want to go out on the bike, Aakash.'

'Why, what's with my bike?'

'I don't want to be seen going out with you.'

'What? Why is that?' I was surprised to hear this after all these days.

'Please don't mind. Somehow my lecturers have got to know about us and have complained about it to my aunt. It's already a huge problem for me trying to convince her that nothing is happening,' she said.

'Okay, I'll get my car.'

'No, please. They will get to know if they see your car.'

'What? Who will get to know?'

'My friends. They know your car. They will tell the lecturers.'

'So what do you want to do? Not go out at all?' I shouted.

'I don't want to risk it,' she said.

Damn you again. What silly reason is that? Sometimes I didn't understand why Aasma acted ridiculous. I couldn't take it further. If she was finding a silly reason not to go out, then there was no point in me coming up with different solutions for it.

***

'Aakash, I hear a lot of things from people about you and Aasma,' Felix said when I met him in the tea shop.

'Well, maybe. People talk a lot about us, so you hear a lot. What is odd in that?' I said as I sat down next to him.

'About Aasma particularly,' he said.

'What did you hear?' I was curious to know, now that he had mentioned her name.

'Not hear but see. I've seen her with Rishab many times while she was going home or near her tuitions. The other day I happened to pass by her tuitions, and I saw her talking to Rishab. Another time I saw them together sitting and talking in their parked vehicle after college. I guess she was on her way home.'

'Why didn't you tell me earlier, Felix?'

'I thought it was nothing important, but I've seen them quite a lot of times, and I thought you should know about it.'

'Well, are you sure it was Aasma?'

'Do you think I don't know Aasma? It was her.'

What I was hearing about Aasma was not good. This prick Rishab was not going to let us alone. Aasma had told me that he was troubling her, but she had not mentioned about him going near her tuitions or troubling her on her way home.

'I'll talk to her about it,' I said. I pretended that it was nothing unusual and that I was cool about it. But deep inside I wanted to do something about him. But I'd have to talk to Aasma first.

***

'Hey, darling. How was your day? Didn't see you at all in college today,' I said when she called me in the night. I had been busy with my computer lab classes and had messaged her that I would be busy with classes.

'Yep, been busy with classes,' she said.

'By the way, I hear things about you.'

'What did you hear now?' She sounded exasperated.

'Did you meet Rishab anytime recently?'

'No. Why do you ask?'

'I hear people seeing you with him near your tuitions and sometimes on your way home. Is he troubling you again?' I asked.

'What can I say, Aakash? If I tell you anything, either you don't understand it or you are ready to pick a fight. So I don't tell you anything at all. He has been troubling me quite a lot.'

'What did he do now? What does he want? I am going to break his neck!' I shouted.

'See, that's why I don't tell you anything!' she shouted back.

'Alright. Tell me what happened,' I asked her, trying to sound calm.

'He follows me every day and tries to talk to me till I reach home. I don't respond to him much. He comes near my tuitions and parks his vehicle right next to me. I can't ask him not to pass by the same street or park his vehicle. He sometimes blocks my way if I don't stop to talk to him.'

'So what do you do then?' I asked, trying to remain calm until I heard everything from her.

'I stop to talk to him for a while or I talk to him near my tuitions.'

Now I understood why she didn't want me to come near her tuitions or why she could not meet me in the evening. She thought I'd pick a fight with Rishab if I saw that. Guess she was right. I would definitely punch him on his nose.

'Listen, Aakash, I don't want you to do anything about it. I can take care of it. I don't want you to worsen it. Please stay away from it.'

'What? How could I do that? Do you think I'm going to let him do that again? I will straighten him up tomorrow morning.'

'Aakash, promise me you will not do anything. Please don't bring me more trouble. I will handle it myself. I will not tell you anything at all or meet you if you do anything.'

***

Next morning I went in search of Rishab with my some of my friends. I wanted to show him his place. I wanted to show him that it would be a mistake if he tried to trouble Aasma again.

We searched for a while, but the lucky bastard was not to be seen anywhere. I had gotten his phone number. I wanted to call him and ask him to meet me. When I called him, I couldn't control myself. I let out all the rage. Instead of asking him to meet me, I had given him all kinds of warnings. I don't remember all that I had spoken. It was all over in a few minutes. I didn't hear what he had responded to my threats.

***

Aasma was not answering my call. I had tried many times already.

She messaged, 'I don't want to talk to you now. I am upset. Please don't call me.'

I called her again, and she answered. Aasma was really upset with what I had done in the morning. She was crying about it. Yes, I had made a scene about it in college. All such news spreads like wildfire in the college campus, and before you know it, you are a hot topic for everybody else to talk about. I had a hard time convincing her that I would not do anything and promised her that

I would let her handle it. It was hard for me to do that. I wanted to kick the brat Rishab until he was no longer able to stand like a man. But I wanted Aasma more than him. I had to let go of it for now. I knew that time would come when I would do it again but with more punches.

**

'Please don't meet me in the campus. My lecturers have seen us together and complained to my parents about it. My parents have asked the college authority to keep a close watch on me. My aunt spoke to my parents. They may come down to Mysore. Am not sure,' she said answering my call. I had called her to check if she could meet me in the complex.

'What new thing is this?' *Why do girls have all these troubles?* I had to ask myself.

'I'll talk to you later, Aakash. I have class now.' She hung up.

**

'What beeping noise is that? Is Saloni calling you again?' I asked. I heard beeps from her phone when we were speaking.

'Yeah, crazy girl,' she said. 'I didn't respond to her message. So she has started to call me. Anyways, my sister wants my phone to talk to a friend. I'll talk to you tomorrow. Don't call me again tonight. My phone will be with my sister.'

'Alright. Love you.'

'Love you too,' she said and hung up.

After a long time, I was watching an action movie that night. With all the action going on in my life, I never felt the need to watch television. Hours later, I felt sleepy. Today's conversation had lasted a few minutes. Well, a few minutes meant an hour or so in my terms. I felt like talking to her again. But I knew her sister would be using her phone. Hoping that Aasma would have her phone back, I called her again. It was too late into the night. Her phone was still busy. How long can somebody use another's phone? Damn her sister. I dozed off.

***

'I don't know who told him I was there. How would I know?' she screamed into the earpiece. Apparently Sam had seen Aasma with Rishab again in the multiplex.

'Were you out with him?' I asked angrily.

'What? No. Why would I go out with him? I was with my cousin,' she said.

I had called her when Sam had told me, and she had not answered my call.

'Then why did you not answer my call? I called you thrice!' I yelled.

'My sister was using my phone. It was with her. Aakash, why are you acting like this? What has happened to you? Nowadays you don't believe me at all. Everything I do, you somehow relate it to Rishab. What have you been thinking?'

She started crying about this. Again the usual drama of me apologizing and trying to convince her went on for hours.

Chapter 16

I n recent times, our relationship was not as healthy as before. Many times we quarrelled about petty things. Many times I did not like what she was doing, and she did not like the way I was taking it. In the past few months, at times we went on for days without talking or without seeing each other. Be it because of examinations or internals or be it because of her tuitions or maybe because we had argued about something and neither one of us was willing to give up. Every time, I was the one to give up. We saw each other less and less in college. We did not meet or spend time together sitting in the cosy complex building or in the café. But I did not mind that as long as I had her with me and we loved each other. Guess that was not needed anymore. Maybe every relationship passed through rough times and this was just one of those times. I knew things would be better tomorrow.

***

After a long time, Aasma agreed to go out with me. I don't know how she agreed to it. I just tried my luck, and she readily accepted. Maybe she wanted it as well. The everyday happenings in our life were taking a toll on our relationship, I guess. I had to arrange for quick money and other stuff. We skipped all the classes and went out for a long drive to the same riverside resort that we had been to. We spent the day in the quiet surroundings and talked about all the things that were happening to us.

That evening, she asked me to meet up. I met her after her tuitions. I saw the brat Rishab there. But I was far enough that he could not see me. It was quite dark in the place where I had parked my car. I didn't know why she had called me.

She sat in the passenger seat of my car. She was quiet for a while. I asked her why she wanted to meet me. It was the first time I was near her tuition institute. First she did not want me near her tuition, and now she called me there and didn't bother to give me a reason.

I took her hand, tightly held it. I guess she had a lot going on in her mind. I asked her to step out for a bit. I went to the other side. I motioned her to come closer. She stepped forward, and I clasped her. Maybe she just wanted to be with me. Maybe she wanted to feel protected. Maybe she just wanted my support. I did not bother to ask her anything. I was just there to give her comfort. And I don't remember how, but that evening we made out in the back seat of my car, and it was a fantastic feeling.

Sometimes it's hard to understand girls. She had not spoken much. But I felt like she was talking a lot over the phone now. Maybe my hug had done some magic on her. I think she wanted to tell me a lot. She was talking and talking, and we spoke until early hours. Finally she stopped when I felt so sleepy that I could not even respond to her.

***

'Hey, sweetie, what are you doing?' I asked when I called her. I had not seen her nor spoken to her all day in college. She was tied up with classes, and I was busy playing snooker all day.

'Am studying, Aakash. I've got internals tomorrow,' she said.

'Oh, how is the preparation going?'

I heard beeps again.

'Going well. I hope I clear it. Wait, I'm getting a call.' She paused to check her phone. 'Saloni it is. Guess she is calling to talk about the subject. I'll have to study now. Can't talk to you. I'll see you tomorrow in college.' She hung up.

What about my internals? I told myself. *I still talk to her if I have internals or even exams. I don't ask her not to call me. Why can't she talk for a while when I can do that for her? Never mind. It's always me who has to give up.*

***

I had been sceptical about Aasma's behaviour lately. What was she tied up with? What was keeping her so occupied recently? We hadn't been meeting up lately. Every time, I got to hear reasons not to meet up or not to go out. In college too, whenever she had time, she made up a reason to go out with friends. She asked me not to meet in college because her aunt had asked the college authorities to keep an eye on her, yet she could skip classes and go out with friends.

Every now and then, her sister used her phone to call her boyfriend or she wouldn't answer my call because her phone was on silent mode. Sometimes she didn't want me to call her at all because she was going out with her aunt.

Her dad had started to call her frequently. Her friends called her up in the middle of the night. And that meant the end of our late-night sweet talks. But her phone continued to be busy until late night.

The frequent arguments about Rishab, her absurd reasons about not being able to meet up or answer my call. Repeated quarrels had started to take their toll on our relationship. There were more arguments than moments of love and affection. I think every relationship is demanding.

***

'Wait, my friend is calling. I'll call you back.' She cut me off in the middle of the conversation. She called back after a while.

'What happened?'

'One of my friends called. I asked her to call later,' Aasma said.

Still I was hearing tic-tac noises. I could make out that she was messaging hastily. Only the hurried click of each button on her phone made such noise.

'Are you messaging someone?' I asked.

'How do you know?'

'I can hear the noise of pushing buttons.'

'Yes, Saloni is messaging me. I'm wearing a hands-free headset so that I can talk to you while I message.'

'Come on, Aasma. Finish off the messaging and then call me. I don't want to hear the rattling noise. It disturbs me,' I said and hung up.

Now I recall that I had heard the noise many times earlier, but I never bothered to ask her. Who was she continually messaging? She called back a while later. I could make out that she was still wearing a headset. The microphone that came with the hands-free headset could pick up the minute noise of her breathing. The noise of buttons being clicked continued in the background. I knew that she was still messaging. But I did not ask her until later on.

She continued to seem disinterested in talking to me and occupied with something else. I could clearly make it out.

'Are you still messaging?' I asked.

'Yes, you said the noise was disturbing you, so I'm messaging from my sister's phone.' She giggled.

Very clever, I told myself. And I ended the conversation quite soon after. She seemed occupied with messaging, and I did not like to continue talking to half-minded Aasma.

CHAPTER 17

I had lost touch with social networking for a while. I checked my profile online, and to my delight, a few girls from our college had sent me friend requests. I wish they had sent me requests before I had met Aasma. I would have been happy to start a relationship with them. Now they were late in doing that. I was no longer interested in them. I didn't respond to their requests. Ever curious, I checked Aasma's profile. It looked to be very active with recent comments and activities even a few hours ago. She had uploaded quite a few of her photos as well. Some of them were from the time she was in Mangalore. I saved all the photos to my computer. It reminded me of the time I met her in Mangalore. I still recall the first time, the first touch, the first date, and the first of everything, and it brought a smile upon my face.

The smile turned to anger when I saw her recent activities. Chat with Rishab. I continued to check the activities of the past month. Aasma was in continuous touch online with Rishab. I did not like it in the least. But I knew what her answer would be if I asked her, or surely we would end up arguing over it and stop talking for another two days. I wanted to avoid that trouble. Though I didn't intend to ask, I decided to keep a tab on it.

In the recent weeks, I had noticed slight changes in Aasma's activities. She was continuously occupied on the phone in messaging.

'My friends are messaging me from class,' she had replied when I had asked. It didn't really bother me at that time, but now I was curious to know who she was chatting with. In fact, I wanted to know if she was chatting with Rishab.

'Are you chatting with Rishab?' I asked.

'What? No. Why would I chat with him?' she replied, not even looking up.

I knew that she was lying. But I didn't want to take it further.

***

'Aasma, what were you doing in the café?' I was angry. I had seen Rishab go into the café. I had been watching the café for a long time. I knew that only Aasma and her friend were in the café. I was pretty sure he was going to meet Aasma.

'What? I was with my friends,' she said.

'Which of your friends were there?' I asked. Her vague answer annoyed me even more.

'I and one of my friends.'

'I know which friend.'

'Then why do you ask if you who know I was with?'

'What has happened to you, Aasma? What was he doing there?'

'He came to talk to my friends, not me.'

Damn you, girl, I told myself and hung up. I knew she was up to something.

***

'Don't you have classes now?' I asked Saloni. I had called her up earlier and asked to meet me in the café.

'No classes today, I guess. You wanted to talk to me. What is the matter?' Saloni asked.

After I had seen Aasma's chat history and Rishab in the movie theatre, I was a little suspicious. I wanted to find out what was happening between Aasma and Rishab.

'Listen, Saloni, I wanted to ask you something. That's why I called you here today,' I said.

'Why do you keep calling Aasma in the night? She tells me that you call her several times during the night. I want to know what is so important that you keep calling her every night,' I asked Saloni, trying to sound casual.

'Me? I don't call her every night. I rarely call her. She would always be busy over a call. Why would I call her so many times, and why during the night? I meet her every day in college. What would I have to talk to her every night? I don't know what Aasma has told you about me, but I don't call her so many times as you think. I know how close you guys are, but believe me, you are not the only guy she talks to, and you are not the only guy she goes out with.'

'What are you talking about, Saloni? What crap are you telling me?' It was hard for me to take in what Saloni was telling me.

'I should have told you this a lot earlier, Aakash, but I didn't want to poke my nose in your business. You must know Rishab from our class. Aasma and Rishab are way closer than you think. They both talk over calls for hours every night. They've been out so many times. Guess you don't know all this. She might be giving you all good reasons about her wanting to spend time with us or her aunt being strict or her dad calling her or even me calling her, but they are all false. She has lied to you so many times right in front of me and has gone out with Rishab. I don't understand why you are such a fool that you didn't know this till now. My humble advice to you is to leave her. I don't want to be the bad person here, but I am telling you the truth. If you don't believe me, you will get to know yourself.'

I couldn't move a muscle. What Saloni had just told me hit me like a rock right across my face. I couldn't move. It was hard for me to digest whatever she told me. I left Saloni without answering anything. I didn't have anything in my defence to tell her. I came home and locked myself in my room and thought about it for a long time. Maybe whatever Saloni told me made sense. The late-night call disturbances, the messages, the new ring, the irrational reasons not to meet me, or her aunt being strict and her sister using her phone to call her boyfriend. The continual tic-tac messaging noise. It all came together now. Every reason she gave me was a lie. All the while, it was Rishab.

***

I did not want Aasma to know that I knew what she was up to. I was furious with her now. But still I did not want to give up on it. Not until I saw it for myself. Till now I had been hearing from others, but never once had I witnessed it myself.

Even though so many things had happened and I was oblivious to it, I trusted Aasma. There had to be a reason for it, a reason for what she had been doing.

I continued to seem as oblivious as possible to everything that was going on, and never did I let her feel that I knew something was unusual. I played along with the sweet talk every night. I stopped questioning about the continual disturbance of her messaging or her middle-of-the-night friend calling. I had become immune to it, I guess, or perhaps I was no longer bothered about it because deep within my mind, I knew the finality of it. Yet I never let my hopes go.

By now, I rarely met her. I was exhausted hearing so many absurd reasons. So many reasons about friends and so many troubles about Rishab that I sometimes had to believe that Rishab was actually blameless. It was not uncommon for us to go without talking to each other for days. The realization struck me like a smack across my face. We had drifted apart. Our relationship was falling apart.

Vachan had seen them go to the movies together once. He had told me immediately. He had no idea what Aasma was up to. My heart sank when he told me. I tried to sound composed and told him that I knew about it and that she had told me that she was going out for a movie with her friends. I tried to pretend that I was fine with it. I know that he did not buy it. But he did not bother going further.

***

Days passed, and I continued to act as if nothing had happened. I wanted the shock of revelation to take her down. More and more our late-night talks were interrupted by friends' calls and an aunt coming to her room to check on her. I knew those were only reasons enough to end the conversation and start a new one with somebody else.

Before long, I asked her out of the blue when I heard the familiar beeping noise amidst our conversation.

'Who is calling you at this time?' I asked, trying to sound as calm as possible, though I had a difficult time holding on to the rage I had inside me.

'I don't know. Some friend,' she said innocently.

'I know it's Rishab. Go ahead. Answer the call.' I was waiting for her reaction. There was a long silence. I could imagine her expression of astonishment. I actually wanted to see her face with that expression.

To my surprise, she said in an evenly composed tone, 'I'll call you back,' and disconnected.

I didn't have to wait long enough for her to call back.

'Yes, Aakash. Tell me,' she said, sounding as if nothing had happened.

'What did he say? Did he ask you not to talk to me? Or did he ask you who you were talking to? Let me guess, maybe you gave him the reason of a cousin calling you from the US,' I said with a wide grin on my face.

'I can't talk to you now. I'll meet you tomorrow.' She disconnected. I sensed that she was about to cry. She did sound like she was about to cry.

It was a long wait for sunrise. I don't know when I slept. I woke up feeling fresh. I don't know for what reason. I took my sweet time getting ready and going to college. I wanted her to wait for me. I knew that she would confess today. I wanted the anxiety to tear through her heart.

Before I left for college, she sent me a message asking me to meet her in the complex. I deliberately reached there way later than she had asked me.

I just stood there like a hero. I wanted her to feel guilty for what she had done and look at what she had lost. She came right to the point.

'Listen, Aakash, I don't know how you got to know about it—' she started to say.

'Why?' I cut her talk short.

'He messages me every night. He calls me every night. If I don't receive his call, he calls the fixed-line phone. My aunt picks up, and he disconnects. I tried disconnecting the fixed line. He said he would come near my home if I tried doing that again. He says that he would take pictures of us together and send it to my parents if I went out with you. That's why I rarely meet you. I always try to see if he is not around when I meet you. He said that he'll tell my family and friends about us and spread rumours about us. He has threatened that he would harm you if he got to know that I met you. I did not want anything to happen to you. I was only trying to protect you all this while.'

I started my bike; I left the place without bothering to answer.

CHAPTER 18

I was contemplating what had happened. I wanted some time alone. I locked myself in my room and listened to my favourite music. I had forgotten my favourite pastime of listening to music all the while.

I recalled every word that she had said. Hope was the only thing I was clinging on to now. I duly hoped that whatever she said was true. I considered it best to give her some space. I will let her take time and resolve the mess that she created, for she had been the reason for it.

***

For two weeks I did not see her nor did I bother to return her numerous calls or messages. After all this while of considerate thought, what Aasma had told me did make some sense. She might have been doing this because Rishab had threatened her. Maybe she was right. I guess I had taken it all to be wrong. Maybe she was right in doing so. My response did hurt her. In spite of everything, I felt sorry for her and I cursed myself for not understanding her feelings and hurting her. I wanted to apologize to her.

I checked the messages from her. She said that she would be going to Mangalore in the next two days and wouldn't be back until the next week.

I thought of talking to her when she returned from Mangalore. I would apologize and make things right for her.

The next morning, I happened to meet Saloni in the college campus.

'Hey, Saloni, how are you?' I asked, walking up to her.

'Hey, Aakash, you look so low. Are you alright?' she asked.

'Am doing just fine. Where is Aasma? I don't see her,' I asked.

'Oh, she must be somewhere with her friends. Have you still not gotten over it yet?'

'No. I mean she told me everything,' I said. 'Everything that happened and about Rishab too.'

'Did she tell you everything?' she asked, looking surprised.

'Yeah. I wanted to apologize to her. I haven't talked to her for over a week. I haven't been returning her calls either. She messaged me that she would be going to her home town tomorrow. I think I'll talk to her after she returns.'

'Apologize? Did she tell you that she is going to Mangalore tomorrow?' she asked, looking even more surprised.

'Yeah, why?' I asked, confused by her reaction.

'Are you out of your mind?' She seemed to be shouting. 'Here. Maybe this will help you.' She passed her phone to me. 'She uses my phone to message Rishab. Go through all the messages. She is not going to Mangalore tomorrow.'

I took the phone from her. I read all the messages. Every message that I opened and read made me feel more and more miserable. Every sentence in the message was like a bullet tearing through my heart. I checked the number to which the messages were sent, and it really was Rishab's. And no doubt the messages were sent from Aasma. I knew her style and language of messaging. It really was sent from Aasma. All this while I had been thinking that it was Rishab who wanted her, but no, it was Aasma who really wanted him.

The messages of hers expressing her attraction to him, her love for him; the meeting time, the call time, everything did perfectly sync with all the lies she had told me. It was really well planned. She truly had an elaborate plan, and she did carry it out well. I skipped to the last few messages. What Saloni had said was right. She was not going to Mangalore. In fact they planned to stay out in a resort for the weekend. It had the name of the resort too.

Did I knock myself out? I brought myself back to my senses. It took me a long time to read through the messages. Saloni was kind enough to let me do it as she silently looked at me. I passed the phone back to her, thanked her for bearing with me for long enough, and left the place.

Coming home and thinking about it, I still did not want to believe that Aasma could do that to me. Until now I had been hearing things from others. No doubt everything perfectly fell into place, pointing that Aasma was untrue. I wanted to see it for myself to believe. I would go to the resort tomorrow. My last hope of proving everybody wrong and standing tall amongst them that my Aasma was right and true. I hoped that everybody was wrong and I was right. The last piece of the puzzle.

I called up Felix and asked him to meet me urgently. I briefed him about the situation and a little background of it. I think he understood that I only needed support now and nothing more. He agreed to go to the resort with me. We had a rough guess of what time we should reach the resort.

**

The next morning, we reached the resort roughly the same time as we expected, about early evening. I saw Rishab's car in the parking lot. I was breathing heavily. All my intuition said was that things were going to be worse. Deep within, I knew the answer. I did not want to give up on it.

Felix had a chat at the reception. He had to shove five hundred bucks to get the room number of the people from that car who had checked in. I don't know what trick he pulled off. The receptionist gave us the name, calling them a couple. *Yeah, couple my arse*, I told myself. Well, as expected, they had used false names. Felix shoved another five hundred bucks to let us stroll around the room they had booked in.

It was a long walk from the reception area. Curse my luck, from a distance, I saw them. Undoubtedly, it was Aasma and Rishab. They stood at the door holding each other. I watched them cuddle and kiss. I watched them close the door behind them.

I had my answer. I knew what would happen next. I couldn't let myself think about it. I was no longer the only person in her life. She had someone more important now. I had lost my worth.

I walked back to the reception area. I guess Felix understood the look on my face. He did not let me drive. He took the car keys from me. Maybe he did the right thing. I would have jumped off the bridge. Our two hours' return drive went without a word. Nearing my home, Felix took the opposite turn and said, 'I'll get you some medicine' and drove straight to the nearest bar and restaurant. Yeah, the right medicine. I got myself drunk until I no longer had the ability to think. Damn if I remember how I got home or who opened the door or how Felix went back to his place.

CHAPTER 19

I woke up the next morning with a terrible headache. The drink was good enough to knock me out, but I needed real medicine to get rid of this headache. I swallowed two aspirins and slept over it for a few more hours.

I woke up feeling fresh in the evening. First thing I did was to call up Felix. I asked him to pick me up on the way to the tea shop. Felix had called up Sam and Vachan already.

I sat on the easy chair out in the garden as I waited for Felix. My phone buzzed. Aasma was calling me. I answered her call.

'Aakash, are you still angry with me?'

'No. Why?' I asked. I felt emotionless, and perhaps I did sound like a robot answering her.

'Then why are you doing this to me? Why haven't you been answering my call? I cried so much,' she said, trying to sound unhappy. She still thought that I didn't know about her trip with Rishab.

'Well, what can I say?' I said. Truth be told, I did not know how to tell her. She had played me well. Congratulations and fuck you at the same time, I wanted to say.

'Aakash, I love you!' she cried out.

I clicked off the phone. That was the last lie I was going to listen to from her. I switched off my phone and sat there looking at the setting sun and listening to the call of the birds. Strangely enough, I felt relieved. A sense of relief that everything was over. A sense of peace. I did not have anything more to worry about. At the same time, I felt terrible to have been through all this. Maybe the emotions were overwhelming to the extent that I did not feel anything at all.

EPILOGUE

'Nikhil, I am thinking about the long and adventurous journey, a lifetime experience that taught me so much about love and life. Back then it was highly unlikely that I would ever see her again unless I pursued the girl who had become the love of my life. She went to Dubai, and I returned to Mysore. I was in a position where I had to make a decision. A decision that would seal the way how my life would be in future. Whether to go behind the girl I loved or move on with life. A choice that would impact my family and my career,' Aakash said. I was jerked out of my imagination when he called out my name.

He continued to say, 'So here I am, Nikhil, after all these years. I did not see her again after that, nor did I ever try to contact her. She still believes that I don't know about her brush with Rishab and that I ditched her for no reason. I shall let her have that pleasure. Now as I think of it, I was foolish enough to fall for it and silly to have believed her. If I have my memory and mathematics right, she had lied to me 119 times. I only told you about a few of them. Now I realize that she had pulled off all classic ways of cheating on me. I was royally fucked.

'It took me a long time to get over it. Years in fact. I'm fortunate enough to have had good friends around me. They never let me stay alone after that. I got detained from college for a year. I left Mysore and stayed with my sister in B'lore in the meantime. It was a much-needed change. Change of environment. Change of people. I had little contact with me people back in Mysore at the time. I had to rewrite all my examinations. I had my focus on clearing my examination and becoming an engineer. I now recognize the importance of spending time with family and friends. The true loved ones. That very day, I promised myself that I would spend my time doing only what I loved to do. And I have done so to date.

'Sometimes I feel good that it actually happened to me. Perhaps that changed the way I look at life. It shaped me into the person that I am today.

'So that's the story of my love in short. What do you have to say?' Aakash asked me.

I said, shaking my head in amazement, 'Kaleidoscopic love.'